Spell Me the Truth

Cat Francis

Copyright © 2018 by Cat Francis

All rights reserved. This book or any portion thereof may not be reproduced or used in any manner whatsoever without the express written permission of the author except for the use of brief quotations in a book review.

Printed in the United States of America

First Printing, 2018

ISBN 978-0-692-13865-6

Keltic Cat Press
PO Box 360392
Hoover, AL 35236

Website: catfranciswrites.bravesites.com

Cover Art Copyright © 2018 by Johnathan Corrales

Dedication

To Becky, who was more beautiful and bright than she ever understood.

To Justine, who believed the best in everyone.

Acknowledgments

Ah yes, Dear Reader, I know you view this page as much the way movie goers view the end credits – if it isn't Marvel, most do not stay. However, for those whose names appear on that roll, it is a very important part of the movie. So, skip ahead if you must. Or maybe there's something at the bottom for you. I don't know… am I a proper nerd?

I would like first to thank my husband, John, for all of his support, talent, and love. His artwork graces the cover of this book. Without his support, I would not have been brave enough to publish.

I would like to thank my friend, Kathy Bright, for both her encouragement and skepticism. She knew I could write, but what she doubted was whether I would be able to stay out of my own way. Writing a novel is messy. You have to be willing to write things that will just be deleted later. You have to be willing to risk typos and grammatical errors, and writing things that are just plain stupid. And yet, writing is the easy part – the hard part is editing. Kathy knows me well enough to know that I don't like to get messy. She knew I am the type of person who edits as I go, and that giving myself the freedom to misspell words and use bad grammar was going to be the most challenging part of this endeavor. (I doubted this as well, to tell you the honest truth.) But when I finished the first draft of this novel, she was probably as proud of me for that success as I was.

I would like to thank my friend, Justine Fernandez. She gave me a beautiful review upon reading the first draft. I only wish she were here to see the finished copy.

I would like to thank my editor, Linda Ullrich. So many of her suggestions are within. If you're looking for an editor, I recommend her.

And, of course, my parents who have supported me in everything – even though I'm sure they will not like this book, as it is simply not a genre they read. That's okay. There's a reason why there are so many different genres out there. They have always believed I could do anything I set my mind to, even when they didn't understand it. I appreciate that because not everyone is lucky enough to have a family who believes in you enough to help you believe in yourself.

I would also like to thank everyone who read this novel in one of its draft formats and gave me feedback – some of that feedback significantly added to the story: Genevieve Carnell, Ali Sciarratta, January Smith, Linda Ullrich, and Amy Weisburg,

I must also acknowledge National Novel Writing Month (NaNoWriMo) for creating the space and incentive for me to write this. November is National Novel Writing Month. It's a space where hundreds of thousands of people set out to do the impossible – write a novel in a month – and succeed. "Spell Me the Truth" started as a NaNoWriMo project, many years ago. It has been through many edits and many titles since that November. However, the missive of NaNoWriMo is that words count. You cannot edit what you do not have on paper. So a huge thank you to the creators of NaNoWriMo for providing the space and support to novelists everywhere. If you've ever wondered "Can I write a novel?" join them in November. You won't know unless you try.

While I've read Tarot cards for a while, it was only since I joined a group that I have become more confident in it.   To the members of the Birmingham Tarot Group, I'd like to thank you for all you have taught me.

To you, Reader, who read all of the names of those who helped me with this book, I thank you. You hold in your hand the culmination of a ridiculous amount of work and procrastination, all to make a dream come true.   Thank you.

Table of Contents

Dedication i
Acknowledgments iii
Prologue 1
Chapter 1 25
Chapter 2 35
Chapter 3 43
Chapter 4 61
Chapter 5 75
Chapter 6 91
Chapter 7 99
Chapter 8 115
Chapter 9 133
Chapter 10 147
Chapter 11 163
Chapter 12 175
Chapter 13 195
Chapter 14 217
Chapter 15 225
Chapter 16 243

Chapter 17 255
Chapter 18 265
Epilogue 283
About the Author

Prologue

The carnival slowly wound its way into the small dark town. It was a relatively small carnival, and quite run down. There were only six rides, most of which were for children. The only ride for adults was a Ferris wheel, which had obviously already seen better days. Its paint was chipping off of the wooden frame. The buckets, once brilliant hues of red, blue and green, were now faded. The circus itself had only a few performers, who were themselves already showing signs that they would need to retire soon.

Still. It was a carnival, and the town was small. It would be exciting enough for people who had to travel thirty miles just to see a movie.

Ruth and Diane were certainly excited as they lay in their window seat watching the carnival's slow approach. The fourteen year old twin sisters were not much alike. Where Ruth had bright red hair and light green eyes, with freckles, and mostly had a somber expression, Diane was fair haired with blue eyes and usually wore a smile. Ruth was adventurous. Diane was shy. Still, they were very close and complemented one another well. They did everything together.

They shared adventures--with Ruth dictating the terms and Diane following along, happy to spend time with her sister. It was not that she didn't enjoy a good adventure, she simply was happy with life as it came and didn't feel the need to seek out thrills.

Ruth was never really satisfied with life in the small town of Cleghorn. She longed to see the world, to see the big city where she could walk for miles and never see anyone she knew. She wanted to see all the dancing and entertainment she often read about. She longed for a life where she could go to the store and buy a book without someone asking her the next day what chapter she was on. Nothing happened in a small town without everyone knowing.

And that was because there was nothing else to do but to get into everyone else's business.

Ruth didn't want to work in a grocery store, or get married right after high school. She wanted to live--and living to her meant adventure. Above all, Ruth wanted the chance to live her life in relative anonymity. She didn't dream of fame or fortune. She dreamt of peace, solitude. Of seeing what was out there and being a part of it.

Diane, though, would be satisfied working at the register of the grocery store. And she already had Kyle, her sweetheart. To Diane, life was best lived at a quiet, slow pace. Kyle was a nice enough boy, for a small-town girl. All of the boys in Cleghorn were nice enough boys for small town girls. And while Ruth lived in a small town, it was never where her heart was. She wouldn't stay in this small town.

Ruth knew that Diane only went along on their adventures because she wanted to keep Ruth happy. That suited her fine. Ruth hoped to awaken a sense of adventure in Diane, so that she'd truly be a part of her life. Diane was also really the only person who accepted Ruth exactly as she was. Diane listened to her dreams of adventure in the world, but she wanted no part of those adventures. She was happy to stay here, in Cleghorn, for the rest of her life, and see Ruth whenever Ruth came home for a visit.

Ruth tried hard to accept Diane as much as Diane accepted her. But it burned. Ruth wanted to share all of this with Diane--the only person she really cared at all about. She tried more and more adventures. But there really was not much a fourteen-year old girl could do in a small town in the middle of nowhere. You could only climb so many trees while pretending to climb cliffs, or scramble across so many streams while pretending to be chased by bandits. There were only so many adventures to be had in a small town. But the world was bigger and offered so much more. Ruth wanted to share it with Diane--and make her really understand what an adventure was.

Father and Mother didn't really understand Ruth either. But that was all right, because they respected that she would leave as soon as she graduated from high school. They knew she wanted to travel and had promised not to try to stop her. They told her she was always welcome to come back home and accepted that she was going to leave as soon as she could. Ruth was already putting all of her allowance towards saving for a car and her parents had promised to match her savings when she was ready to buy. The car was her ticket out.

But in the meantime, there was something exciting happening in Cleghorn for once. A carnival, a real adventure...and Ruth, for one, could hardly wait.

When the sun came up, Ruth and Diane got ready for school. Ruth enjoyed the classes, knowing she was learning about the world she was destined to meet. So she paid attention in geography and kept a diary of the places she would visit. And she listened closely in history and lit, to find out where the interesting stuff happened. Diane barely tolerated it. Ruth couldn't really blame her. After all...she didn't really need a lot of knowledge of geography to run a register over at the Piggly Wiggly. There was not a lot of opportunity here in Cleghorn. She could work at the bank, the feed store, the gas station, or the Piggly Wiggly. But Ruth kept Diane sharp on her studies--hoping that if she studied enough, Diane would get a taste for the world outside and want to join her. Ruth still had four years to convince Diane to come with her and Ruth wanted to make sure her sister was ready too. Just in case.

As they walked to the school, Ruth looked around hoping to see where the carnival was set up. It was all she could talk about. Ruth had read books about characters who had gone to carnivals and here was one coming into her life. For once, she was going to get to experience something she had only read about. She just knew it would somehow change her life. And she couldn't wait.

Would there be elephants or tigers at the circus? What kind of games would there be? And she had seen a Ferris wheel driving by, Ruth was sure of it, and she had always wanted to ride one. To sit high above the town and gaze out for miles around her, higher than the tree tops. That would be wonderful.

"What do you think the town will look like from the Ferris wheel?" Ruth asked Diane. Diane shrugged, not at all interested in the Ferris wheel. But Ruth kept talking about it.

"I'm not riding it," Diane said suddenly. It was unusual for her to not agree with one of Ruth's plans,

Ruth's adventures, especially one as innocuous as this one. Unusual? No, it was unheard of. Diane never disagreed with Ruth.

"What?" Ruth asked. She was a little surprised that Diane was opposed to something she was this excited about.

"I'm not riding it."

"But why?"

"I don't like heights. I never have."

"But you climb trees with me all the time!" Ruth said, a bit surprised by Diane's refusal.

"For you, but I don't like them. And a tree is solid and fairly close to the ground. That thing is not natural, and I didn't like the look of it. I'm not riding it." Diane was adamant.

Ruth nodded, extremely disappointed. "Would you at least wait until you see it? I mean, maybe it won't look so bad when it's put together. Okay?"

Diane looked at her a minute. "I will give it a look. But I'm making no promises that I will ride it. That's the best I can do."

Ruth smiled and hugged her sister. "That's all I can ask."

Diane looked in the mirror at her sister. Ruth normally didn't put a lot of effort into her appearance. Yet, here she was, fussing over shirts, trying to find one that best matched her eyes. She had on her good jeans. Finally, Diane gave up on Ruth and went to Ruth's closet and pulled out a bright green button-down shirt with short sleeves and a black belt. "Here. This looks good on you." Diane was already dressed in a blue top with ruffles, a matching blue belt, and jeans.

Ruth smiled. "Thanks. I want to look good."

Diane shrugged. "I don't see why. The only people there who you don't already know are the carnies. And they aren't going to stay around. Unless there's a boy you have your eye on that you haven't mentioned."

"No. I just want to look just right," Ruth said. Even she didn't quite understand why it was so important that she look good today. But it was very important to her. Ruth put on the shirt and belt. She brushed out her long hair and put it back in a ponytail. "How do I look?"

Diane smiled. "You look great."

Ruth smiled at Diane. "Thanks, sis. I love you."

"Love you, too. Let's go. I'm sure Mom and Dad are waiting for us."

Ruth nodded and headed out of their room. Diane followed close behind. Downstairs, their parents were waiting for them. Mom was wearing a dress. Dad was in his suit. Ruth grinned.

"Ready, girls?" Father asked.

Both of them nodded. Ruth was fairly bouncing and Diane was also very excited. After all, this was the first time a carnival had ever come to their town. It was sure to be crowded. The whole town would be there, and the carnival would only be here today.

Ruth and Diane climbed into the back of the Ford pick-up and their parents got in the cab. The twins waved at their friends as they rode to the carnival. Already, there were a lot of cars in the field.

Ruth could see the lights of the Ferris wheel shining. Oh, she could hardly wait to ride it. She looked over at Diane with a huge smile as they got out of the truck.

"Are you ready?" Ruth asked. Their parents didn't want them running off, so they stuck with them. All of their friends were also pretty tethered to their parents.

"Absolutely!" Diane said with a smile.

Kyle waved as he walked past with his parents and Diane blushed as he mouthed 'you look beautiful' across the way. Their parents didn't yet know that Kyle and Diane were dating--had been dating for a year now. However, Father wouldn't allow either Ruth or Diane to go on any dates until they reached fifteen. And they had three months still to go for that.

They walked to the carnival. The tin music wafted through the air, filling them with anticipation. It sounded a bit flat and mechanical, but it was still thrilling. And the smells. Popcorn, but it didn't smell quite like the popcorn they bought at the movies. And sugar. And hot dogs. And a whole lot of things they couldn't identify, but were dying to try.

Ruth wanted to go to the Ferris wheel first. It was at the farthest point of the carnival. Diane shook her head. At this distance, she was quite unsure she wanted to ride it. In fact, she was pretty certain she did not want to ride the rickety looking thing.

So she dragged back, looking at everything, making Ruth squirm with impatience. They played games and won cheap stuffed animals.   Father bought both of them cotton candy, while mother had a candied apple and he had a caramel apple. They went to the small circus. And finally, they arrived at the Ferris wheel.

It was old. The wood looked weathered. It could use at least one coat of paint. The wheel creaked as it turned. And it turned out that the Ferris wheel was the source of the tin music that pervaded the carnival.

Diane blanched looking at the wheel, and shuddered. There were people on it, smiling. But it gave her a very bad feeling. The operator was a short man. His hair was obviously dyed black with shoe black. It was tied back with a ribbon and looked greasy. He wore a top hat made of faded crushed velvet, worn through in several places. His jacket had tears and his shirt had grease stains, as did his hands.

When he looked at them, his eyes were dead. Diane took a step back.

"No, I'm not riding that," Diane asserted. "Definitely not riding that."

Ruth looked at her and then looked at her father. "You know the rule. You can't ride alone."

"Will you ride with me, then, Dad? Please?"

He looked at it and frowned. "No, I don't think so."

Ruth looked to her mother, who also shook her head.

She nearly burst into tears. She was standing at the foot of the Ferris wheel and she couldn't ride. Anger boiled under the surface of her thoughts. This was not fair. She glared at Diane, then softened her look. "Please." She pleaded with Diane.

Diane looked again at the Ferris wheel, then the operator and shook her head. "I'm sorry. But I'm not riding that...that thing."

She had never denied Ruth an adventure before. Diane always went along with Ruth's ideas. Always. And tonight, when it was more important to Ruth than anything else she had ever asked of her sister, Diane refused.

"I'll tell Dad about Kyle!" Ruth hissed. She hated threatening Diane, but she couldn't see any other way she was going to get on that ride.

Diane looked struck a moment. But she recovered to negotiate. "If you want me to ride, tell me why this is so important to you. Tell me that and I'll ride it."

Something in Diane's tone struck Ruth. If she could articulate her need, Diane would have a change of heart and ride for her. But Ruth couldn't explain it. She didn't know herself. She just felt her destiny depended on her riding that Ferris wheel. She opened her mouth and started to say something, but no words came out. She looked down, frustrated with herself...angry at her family, angry at things she just didn't understand.

"I'm really sorry, Ruth. Really, I am," Diane said softly. "I'm sorry," she whispered again as Ruth nodded sullenly.

But their relationship had changed. Irrevocably. Over one ride at an inconsequential carnival in the middle of nowhere. Because one sister had refused to ride a Ferris wheel. And the other had threatened to tell her secret.

The rest of the evening was spent in silence for Ruth. She did not smile when Diane won a goldfish, nor laugh as their father aimed for the bell (and missed abysmally). Diane had fun the rest of the evening, but was concerned about Ruth--almost concerned enough to change her mind about the Ferris wheel. Almost.

Later that night, after everyone was asleep, Ruth snuck out of the house. It was not the first time she had ever done so. It was just the first time she had done so without Diane. She crept along the lane, ducking out of the way whenever she spotted the lights of an oncoming vehicle. Ruth didn't want anyone knowing what she was doing. But she was going to go back to that carnival and she was going to beg the operator to let her ride the Ferris wheel.

It took her an hour to walk there and she was surprised to see him standing beside his wheel.

"I have been waiting for you," was all he said as he opened up the hinge to a bucket. Ruth nodded and climbed in.

The ride was exhilarating. The wheel turned round. And round. Backwards and forwards. Time seemed to stop and the clouds almost moved backwards. Ruth watched it all in amazement. She could feel herself changing--changing in small ways that she didn't understand. Not yet. But she felt like a seed was being planted within her - a seed of what, she didn't know. And if she had known, she would probably have accepted it anyway, regardless of the consequences. She felt more complete and alive than she had ever felt. It was not from the views from the Ferris wheel, like she had believed it would be. And she started to understand that her need to ride really was destiny. Ruth was changing. She watched as the operator stood intent over the controls, seemingly imbuing them with power.

The first light of dawn shone over the horizon, as her bucket paused at the top. Ruth soaked in the first rays of the sun. Then the bucket was lowered and she stepped off. Thanking the man, Ruth realized she had to get home before she'd be missed. She turned back to him, to wave, only to find that the entire carnival was gone and she was standing in an empty field, with nothing there but crushed weeds to show that there had been anything at all occupying the field only a few moments before.

She shook her head and began to walk home, hoping that she could make it before anyone noticed her absence. She had not gone more than ten paces when she came upon her house. It had taken her an hour to get to the field, and thirty seconds to get home. That was strange, but Ruth was not inclined to question it at this time. The sun was still rising slowly and there was a feeling of possibilities in the air. She quickly snuck back in and went into the bathroom, where she had stashed her pajamas. Changing clothes, she glanced into the mirror.

Her eyes had changed. They were brighter...greener. Ruth shook her head a moment then went to the bedroom. She climbed into bed and covered up, just as the alarm rang.

Ruth sat up, as she would if she were just getting up. Diane was looking at her. For some reason, it made her angry. But she kept her silence.

"Good morning," Diane said with a smile.

Ruth said nothing. Diane frowned, but got ready for school. By the time they were ready, Ruth still had said nothing to Diane, and she was liking this feeling. She resolved to continue it.

They walked to school in silence. Diane tried to start conversations and Ruth ignored her. She liked this feeling of power. Diane deserved this, anyway, Ruth thought. She was still angry with Diane for not riding the Ferris wheel. Had Diane ridden with her during the carnival, Ruth wouldn't have been changed. And Ruth didn't know how she felt about that. Was it a good thing or a bad thing? These changes that she was experiencing now should have been for both of them. But Diane was too much of a coward.

Ruth realized that Diane didn't deserve them and she was glad Diane had refused her.

Diane didn't deserve her either. Ruth smiled at this thought. It was true.

Diane walked across the stage and took her diploma. Her parents smiled at her. She watched as her sister, Ruth, also got her degree. She was so glad to see this day happen. Kyle had proposed last night and she had accepted. But she was even more glad because in the parking lot of the school sat Ruth's car, already packed. As soon as this ceremony was over, her sister would be driving off--to who knew where.

It couldn't happen a moment too soon.

For four years, Ruth had not said one word to her, had not smiled at her. Ruth had been very distant. She had grown colder and colder. And her eyes had turned brighter and brighter. Once Ruth's green eyes had been beautiful, now they looked poisonous.

In short, Diane was afraid of her sister. She could almost not remember how close they had been. All she had known was living with a hostile presence, barely contained, for the past four years. When she broke her arm riding her bike, Diane was certain that Ruth was behind it - although Ruth had been nowhere near her at the time. Diane knew it was crazy, paranoid. But she still felt that way.

And she missed her sister. Ruth had changed so much, seemingly overnight. Diane wished she knew what it was, how it had happened and how she could help. At first, she had tried. But Ruth had rebuffed her with silence. Speaking to their parents had been unhelpful. Ruth went out of her way in their parents' presence to not show any difference in behavior. But Diane knew differently, and after a while she gave up trying.

So she was looking forward to this day--the day when Ruth would drive off into the sunset, hopefully never to return.

Kyle smiled at Diane as they stood on the wrap-around porch of their beautiful two-story home in Taylor's Falls. It was their first house. Kyle had been transferred here. He was managing a new Piggly Wiggly and had gotten quite a good raise with the promotion. It was enough that they could afford to buy a home. It was also enough that they could consider raising a family of their own, without Diane having to work.

Life was perfect--as was this house.

The moving van pulled up, and shortly, their meager belongings were being loaded in. Diane directed the movers as they brought in furniture and boxes. She practically glowed with excitement. Diane could hardly wait to get the boxes unpacked and set up their home. Kyle just wanted it done, but he was happy to see his wife so excited.

Diane's parents had both died this past year. Her father had suffered a massive heart attack at the factory and died before the ambulance could arrive. Her mother had been in a fatal car accident less than a month later. The authorities had said she was distracted, probably by grief, and didn't see the road turning away from the ravine. Kyle worried about Diane because she had blamed her sister for both deaths - even though they had not seen Ruth since high school graduation.

Besides, how could Ruth have caused those deaths? Much less, why would Ruth want her parents dead?

Kyle figured it was just that Diane couldn't accept her parents' deaths and needed someone to blame. He thought it was that she had never accepted Ruth's abandonment. Still, a change of scenery would do them both good. And with no other relatives who needed to contact them, there really was no reason for them to leave a forwarding address, which was what Diane wanted.

Diane certainly didn't want Ruth to be able find them. She was convinced that Ruth would be coming after her next. So if it made Diane feel safe, Kyle had no problem with the request.

They got the house organized. Diane had picked out harvest gold appliances for the kitchen and put wallpaper up with autumn leaves. He thought it looked homey. The rest of the house had been rather plain, too. She had opted for hardwood flooring with area carpets, rather than the wall to wall shag he had wanted. But Kyle found that it too was comfortable. The house was decorated very tastefully, and well within their budget.

Diane had also asked him to hang a swing in the giant oak tree in their front yard and Kyle fully planned to do so after the leaves fell. He was going to hang two swings and maybe build a tree house. He knew it was early for a tree house, but why not. He would have more time before they had a child than afterwards. He would stain it to protect the wood for now, and wait to paint the tree house until the children came. Still, a tree without leaves was easier to build in than one that had leaves. He could better see which branches were good and which ones needed to come down. And he wouldn't have to clear leaves out of his way. Nature would have taken care of that already.

In short, their house was everything they wanted. He could see them growing old together here and it made him smile.

Diane gave a start as a long black limo pulled up the driveway. He looked at her. "Someone from corporate here to welcome you?" she asked hopefully.

"I don't know, hon. I wasn't expecting anyone."

Diane frowned as the car stopped. The chauffeur got out of the car and approached the passenger side. He opened the door. The first thing they saw was a high black heel on a well-manicured foot. The foot belonged to an impeccably dressed woman wearing black, with an enormous black hat and dark sunglasses. Diane looked at him. She was worried. Kyle didn't recognize her.

Then the sunlight hit her hair. It was a vibrant red.

As she stepped onto the porch, Diane said "Hello, Ruth."

Ruth smiled at her.

"Hello, Diane. How are you doing?"

Diane didn't respond immediately. It had been a very long time since Ruth had spoken to her at all. "How did you find me?"

Ruth looked taken aback. "Were you hiding from me, sister dear?"

Diane shook her head. "Of course not. But we did just move."

Ruth smiled. "I know. And it's a lovely house. I wanted to visit you and tell you I'm sorry for how I behaved in high school. I missed out on having a sister because I was stupid. Can you forgive me?"

Diane wanted to. She had missed her sister. But she also was unsure. Ruth looked very different, maybe she had really changed. "I want to, Ruth." She looked at Kyle. "You remember my husband, Kyle?"

"Oh you got married. I'm happy for you. I'm sorry I missed it." Ruth paused "But considering that

I was not speaking to you...to anyone really, I'm not surprised you didn't invite me."

Diane started to relax. Soon the two sisters were talking like they had never stopped. Diane was happy and Kyle was thrilled she had her sister back. Diane invited Ruth into the house and gave her the grand tour. Ruth commented on each and every room.

But no one noticed that she left at least one drop of water in each room she was shown. In some rooms, she left more.

Finally, Ruth said, "I'm sorry. I simply must head home."

"Are you sure you don't want to stay the night? It's rather late," Diane said.

"Oh no, I actually live rather close by. That's how I found out you were here, you see. I realized it was a sign that I should apologize. I had been thinking of it for a while. And it just seemed as if this was the universe's way of telling me that it was time. You'll have to come visit me next. I'll call you and send George to bring you."

Diane smiled at this.

"Before I go, please let me give your home a blessing." At Diane's nod, Ruth continued, "Let no dishonesty or deception live here. Only truth shall reside under this roof." Ruth smiled at them and stepped outside of the house and onto the porch. "I'll see you later, sis. I wish you the best and I hope you're happy here."

As Ruth got into the limousine, she turned back to her sister and took off her sunglasses. Diane didn't see her eyes, but if she had she would have noticed that the brightness had not dimmed any. Ruth's eyes were still quite frighteningly bright.

That night, Kyle had a dream. He was touring the tree house that he had built. It was two stories, undecorated except for the wood stain that he had used to protect the wood. It was accessible by ladder. The swings hung down. The backyard was everything he had imagined.

He dreamed that he was pushing Diane on the swings as she laughed gaily. Then suddenly she was flying, higher than imaginable...than possible. She'd somehow released from the swing while it was high and she was free falling. Kyle ran, trying to catch up with her, trying desperately to catch her before she landed. But he arrived a split second too late. Diane fell, hitting her head on a stone. He rolled her over. Her eyes had glazed over, and there was a splash of blood on her forehead. He checked for her pulse. There wasn't one. Kyle pulled her to him, rocking her and sobbing. There was nothing he could do. His beautiful wife was gone.

Kyle woke up with almost a scream. Then he realized it had been a dream...a nightmare really, but still. It wasn't real. He looked over in the bed to check on Diane, but she was not there. That was rather odd.

"Diane?" Kyle called as he got up. His need to see her was almost as intense as his dream. He needed to see that she was all right, that his dream was just that. He walked through the house. She was not in the bathroom. Diane was not in the house. This was even stranger. He would have expected that she would have woken him if she felt the need to go outside.

Still, Kyle walked outside. He was stunned to see two swings hanging from the tree. Swings he had not installed. And there was the two-story tree house, exactly like he had dreamed it.

Kyle began to run, screaming "Diane!" He looked over to where she had died in his dream, hoping and praying that this wouldn't also be true.

He saw a mass of white cloth and ran faster. It was Diane, lying crumpled on the ground, with a splash of blood on her forehead. Kyle checked her pulse. There was none.

Kyle pulled her to him, rocking her and sobbing. But there was nothing he could do. His beautiful wife was dead. Just as he had dreamed.

And he had only one thought. Somehow, Ruth had done this.

The next day, he listed the house for sale and quit his job. He waited until after the funeral to pack up and leave. And that was the last time anyone in Taylor's Falls saw the owner of the white house on the hill.

A few people looked at the home, but it was weird. No one would buy it. Eventually, the home was foreclosed upon. And it sat vacant.

For eighteen years.

Chapter 1

Patricia Smith, known as Patty to her friends, frowned as Madame Ann Dewers, her mentor, laid out a Tarot spread. Patty looked at the spread in front of her mentor. When she first started with any spread, Patty always liked to see the picture as a whole before reviewing the individual cards. This particular spread was full of Swords. Patty had never liked the suit of Swords. Certainly, it was about mental abilities, but it also felt very violent. She knew that cards were neither positive nor negative. However, the reactions that she had to certain cards were definitely strong. Yet, there were also a few cards that she had no reaction to at all.

However, the spread that was on the table evoked negative feelings, and Patty could not figure out why. She focused on the Five of Pentacles. That one made her feel that there was some emotional distance. She saw the Three of Swords next to it, and felt like it meant heartbreak or betrayal. The Six of Swords. Someone was stealing away in the night. Eight of Swords. There was a trial and someone would be trapped.

Perhaps Patty's unease was because she was not looking forward to telling Ann that when the summer ended, she would not have time to continue her lessons. Her school work was going to be very intense this year, and she wanted to do well in her classes. While Patty had a few dear friends, she wanted out of this town.

Here in Taylor's Falls, Patty would always be "oh, poor Patty Smith, that weird orphan." She wanted to be able to escape that reputation and be known for herself, not for her lack of parents. And not where everyone knew who the weird kid was--the one who occasionally had visions and told you about them.

Patty now knew not to tell people about those visions, but when they had first started, she had been very young and had not known it was unusual. So now she was the weird one. The poor orphan.

And yes, she would definitely miss her friends.

But she had to focus. Her grades were good, but Patty had to get into college. More than that, Patty had to get a scholarship. She did not have parents who would help her pay her way. After graduation, she would lose the home she had grown up in. This was her last year to get everything in order, so that she could apply to colleges next year.

And that meant that there were some things she had to sacrifice. Learning from Madame Ann was one of those things.

"You are very distracted today," Madame Ann said suddenly and sharply.

Patty jumped. "You're right." She looked at her mentor. "Summer's almost over."

"Yes. I suppose you're wanting to go spend some time with your friends now."

Patty shrugged. "That, and--"

Madame Ann raised her left eyebrow and stared at her intently. "And?"

"Madame Ann. I...I can't continue our lessons. You have to know how much I appreciate everything you've taught me. I..."

"If you do not learn about your gift, your power, it will overtake you," Madame Ann insisted.

Patty nodded. "I know. But I just won't have time. This is my last year, Madame Ann. I've got to put my efforts into my studies."

Madame Ann frowned, and for a moment, Patty felt menace coming from her. But that could not be right. Ann was a very gentle person, she was probably just very upset that her student was leaving her.

"You are to take over for me when you graduate. You are to be my apprentice," Madame Ann insisted. "This is important! More important than math and science. Bah!"

Patty frowned. "No. I don't want to stay here. I thought you knew that."

"You will stay here," Madame Ann said certainly.

"I'm sorry," Patty said, and she stood up. "I really am. But this is not who I want to be. I want more than to be the town fortune teller. And I know as well as you do that you're more than that. But they look at you, and me, like we're not worth anything."

"They know nothing!" Madame Ann said.

"And I know this is your dream, your happiness," Patty said. Then she looked at Madame Ann. "But it is not mine. It never has been."

"Go!" Madame Ann insisted. "And when you change your mind, you come back. We will carry on then."

Patty nodded and grabbed her sweater and bag. She didn't quite run out the door, but she left as quickly as she could. She felt awful; she had hurt Madame Ann's feelings. Still, that conversation was never going to be easy.

She just wished it had not been that hard.

Patty got on her ten-speed and pedaled from Madame Ann's house toward town. She took the longer route, just because she wanted to ride the rolling hills to work off a little more of her nervous energy. While she was riding, Patty noticed that a car was parked in front of the white house on the hill.

"Strange," she thought. The house on the hill had not been occupied in a very long time.

Still, maybe the person who moved there would be nice and could be her friend. She and her friends had always wanted to see the inside of that place.

About fifteen minutes later, Patty pulled onto Main Street. She had been biking at a relaxed pace. She parked in front of the book store and went right in.

As the bell rang, the owner looked up. "Afternoon, Patty. How are you?"

"Okay, Annabelle. Chessie about?"

Annabelle grinned. "In her usual spot."

Patty smiled and walked to the back of the store, where a very comfortable overstuffed chair was located. Curled up on the chair was a beautiful calico cat. "Hi Chessie."

Chessie murped at her, then stood up and stretched before coming over for a head scratch. Patty had had a frustrating day. "How you been, girl?" Patty asked as Chessie moved over so the girl could join her in the chair, then the cat curled up on Patty's lap. Patty absently pet her as she thought about the day.

Patty was very saddened that she had hurt Madame Ann's feelings. But she was also coming to a point in her life where she realized that there were decisions she had to make for herself. And some of those decisions would hurt other people. The trick was making decisions for the right reasons. Her decision to stop her lessons with Madame Ann had not been made to hurt Madame Ann. That was a consequence of the decision, but not the reason for the decision. The reason was because Patty herself needed to break free and spend more time on her lessons and with her friends. She did not have the time required for her studies with Madame Ann as well. And while she might have been able to continue her visits with the fortune teller, Patty would not have been able to devote time to the lessons Madame Ann was teaching her in preparation for her future visits.

Patty did not like feeling that her decisions would hurt others. But that was how things were. Leaving Taylor's Falls would hurt her friends, whom she left behind; however, the reason she was leaving was not to hurt them. As long as her decisions were not made with ill intent, Patty felt she would be able to learn to live with hurting people whom she cared about. She could communicate with them that she didn't want to hurt them.

They could either accept that, or not. But she could not live her life without hurting other people. No one realistically could.

Chessie looked into Patty's eyes and purred. Then she nuzzled the young lady. Patty hugged her. "Thanks, Chessie. I always feel better when I think something through while I'm petting you."

Chessie licked Patty's arm, then jumped onto the floor to walk off to another part of the book store. "Needed elsewhere, eh Chessie?" Patty said with a smile. The cat looked over her shoulder back at Patty, then winked and walked off.

Patty shook her head and smiled. She went back to the front.

"Chessie help you get sorted out, Patty?" Annabelle asked.

Patty nodded. "You probably should charge for her services."

Annabelle laughed. "I know. But, I suspect most people could not afford her if I did. So, it's best to keep her free to let her decide who to help."

Patty smiled.

Annabelle said, "Oh, I found a book I thought you'd like."

"Really?" Patty had heard Annabelle occasionally picked out books for people, and they usually really liked them.

"Yeah. Here it is," Anabelle reached under the counter and brought up an old book. Patty was surprised. She was expecting maybe a romance or some silly new novel that was all the rage.

"Blessings of the Trees," Patty read softly. Then she looked back up at Annabelle. Patty looked back down and opened up the front cover. A little bit of dust fell as she opened the book. It was old. Patty read the table of contents, and it was a book she would want to read, and keep as part of her personal library. It was also a book she was not in a position to buy right now. "Annabelle, this is a great book, and you're right. I would love it. I just can't af--"

Annabelle interrupted her. "I found it for you. It came in a box of old books. No charge, okay?"

Patty nodded. She was not sure what to say. "Thank you," Patty whispered. Annabelle was one of the few adults who did not treat her like a freak, and Patty did not believe for one minute that Annabelle was trying to make fun of her with this book. This looked like a book she would use. A book of blessings. You could always use blessings.

"Any time. And Chessie is always here for you, if you need a friend or therapist. I'd help out too, but I suspect that a purring cat is always more enjoyable company than an old woman."

Patty laughed. "You're good company too, Annabelle. But I do love cats. I've never tried to have a pet. I suspect the answer would be no."

"Never know until you ask," Annabelle said.

Patty nodded.

Chapter 2

Amilou Polowski looked at her father and asked, "Why did you buy this place again, Dad?" She was in the kitchen, soaking wallpaper so old and decayed that its original pattern was no longer discernable, preparing to remove it when it was soaked enough. Her long blonde hair was pulled back into a rough pony tail, just to keep it out of her way as she worked. Normally, Ami dressed very neatly, but today she dressed for comfort and making a mess, wearing clothes reserved for the messiest of household chores.

The kitchen was very dated, with harvest gold appliances, which no longer worked. New appliances were being delivered tomorrow and the old ones would be removed. But her dad had asked her to take care of the wallpaper first. So here she was in the kitchen, soaking wallpaper.

"The house is great. It just needs a little bit of paint and cleaning. Trust me, Ami. This place will be great once we have it all cleaned up." Jan Polowski loved to find and restore the inner beauty in inanimate objects. This was just the latest in a long line of projects. She hoped, however, that once he had restored this house to its future glory, he would be happy to settle down. If Jan Polowski could buy a house that was ready to live in or one that needed to be 'loved,' he would always choose the one that needed just a little bit of work. She really wouldn't have her father any other way.

"Besides. Did you see that tree house? It's amazing. I'll have someone check it out to make sure it's sturdy, then I'll restore it for you. You can have a club house or whatever you kids call that these days."

Ami sighed. She reached up and pulled one of the strips of wallpaper. It came down in one piece, much to her surprise.

"Good job, Ami!" her dad called in.

"Yeah," Ami thought. "One down." She looked around the room and counted the number of remaining strips. Eight. The first had taken her four hours. Great. She moved down the counter to the next area and started over.

Still, it could be worse. Fortunately, the previous owners had painted all of the other rooms, so it was just a matter of scrubbing down the walls. Her father had tasked her with wall paper removal in the kitchen. He had assigned himself the unenviable task of scrubbing those walls. After the walls were scrubbed, they would both paint all the walls of this house, and then her father would refinish the floors. They had two weeks before the moving truck would arrive with the bulk of their stuff, so they were staying in a hotel while they restored this house.

Her father had always loved to do these things, and had always wanted to renovate a house from top to bottom. Ami smiled. A clubhouse, he had said. Did the kids in this town even use those? School started the week after they got their stuff. She was already registered for her classes. But truly, she was a little nervous. At Memorial, she'd been on the cheer squad and would have been captain this year, if Jan had not been transferred. She had finally gotten enough experience in the theatre department that they were willing to trust her with the major roles. And she had had friends. Friends whom she missed.

"Can we order a pizza, Dad?"   Ami shouted down the hall as she sopped some suds onto the wall. She wanted to stop this train of thought before it went any further and she became depressed. It was all well and good for her father to get a new job in a new town. But she was happy where they were. She had a life, and he had completely disrupted it. Jan had not been the same since Sofia, her mother, had passed on. He never forgot that Ami was around. No, he was a most attentive father. But he did impulsive things, like applying for a transfer within his company, without really thinking about how it would affect her.

"Pizza?" He walked down the hall. "Wanna come with me?"

Ami looked at the wall and frowned. If she left it now it would just dry up, and she'd have to start again. "Nah, I should stay here and work on this. I'll be okay." Besides, she needed a little bit of time alone.

"Okay. Well. I promise to be quick. Pepperoni and sausage, or do you want taco pizza this time?"

"Pepperoni and sausage is good. And we'll need napkins. Could I get a Diet Pepsi? Or Diet Coke. Whatever they have?"

Jan frowned at her. "You don't need to drink diet sodas. You're a beautiful girl and you're not overweight."

Ami sighed. "I know, Dad. You love me just as I am. And I'm not on a diet, all right. If I were, would I have asked for pizza?"

He thought about that for a moment and nodded. "Fair enough. I'll be right back."

Ami nodded. She walked over to her bag and took out her Walkman. Actually, it was an AIWA. Jan had said those were better quality than the Sony. She didn't actually care, so long as she could play her INXS and Foreigner tapes. She smiled as she took out a mix tape her friend Bethany had given her before they left Santa Fe. "Best Friends Mix" she had called it. Ami had already listened to it several times in the week since she left Santa Fe. With Jan out of the house, she could sing to her heart's content.

She put her head phones on, clipped the Walkman to her jeans, and pressed play. She grinned as she heard the first song's beat "Wild Wild West." It was the kind of song she'd prefer to dance to, but it would provide a good rhythm to work on the wall. But, instead of singing the words to the song, she started making up her own as she worked on the wall. It was a quirk of hers. Weird Al Yankovic was one of her favorites, just because he did the same thing to songs as she did.

Forty-seven fall leaves painted on the wall sleeves
North east west south all in the same house
Sitting in a back room waiting for the big boom
I'm in the kitchen washing all the walls down

It's so old but I don't care
I love this house and its wild wild flair
Dance to the beat that we love best
Heading for the nineties
Living in the wild wild west
The wild wild west

Daddy at the parlor pickin up a pizza

Pepperoni sausage maybe with some 'chovies
Forty-seven heartbeats beating like a drum
Got to live it up live it up
Maybe he'll pick up some gum

Now put your flags in the air and march them up and down
You can live it up live it up all over the town
And turn to the left, turn to the right
I don't care as long as we have pizza tonight
Heading for the nineties living in the eighties
Screaming in a back room waiting for the big boom

Give me give me wild west
Give me give me easy paper
Give me love give me love
Give me time to live it up

Ami actually hoped that Jan would take a little while. She did love her dad, but she'd been with him nearly constantly since they left Santa Fe. They shared a double room at the hotel, so she couldn't really listen to her music the way she wanted to. Whenever he went somewhere, she went with him. Ami was actually surprised that he had allowed her to stay here alone, especially since they didn't actually know anyone in this town yet. Besides, even if they did, the phone wouldn't be connected until tomorrow, so she couldn't call anyone. But this was a nice, quiet town.

At the end of the song, Ami decided to give the wall paper a try, and tugged on it. It also came down. So that was two done, and plenty still to go. She kept up with her music, singing her own words about moving and painting and removing wallpaper as she danced on the countertops, keeping an eye out for Jan as she did it. It wouldn't do for her father to catch her in a moment of silliness. He might want to join in, and Ami was not sure she was ready to see Jan be completely silly just yet.

As the music continued, Ami did think some more about school. The wall paper didn't really take much thought, not really. It gave her a little time to brood. She wanted to have some good friends, and she only hoped that there would be some who lived close to her--friends who would want to hang out in her club house, who would invite her over.

Before long, a third piece of wallpaper was down. This was amazing! She had already done three of the nine strips in the kitchen. "This is not bad at all," Ami said. "This paper practically peels itself off!" She reached up and pulled a piece she had not even soaked yet, and it came off as she pulled. Ami decided to try another piece. This one also came off easily. It was so easy, in fact, that she was on the last piece when Jan arrived with the pizza.

He walked in the kitchen and looked around in shock. Ami turned off her music and took her headset off. "I'm impressed!" Jan said. "I expected at most you might have one more piece down, but the whole kitchen?"

Ami smiled. "I know! It was a lot easier than I expected."

"Why don't we wipe down these walls after lunch, and then go out to Sam's Hardware. I'll let you pick out the color of the kitchen walls."

"Really?!" Ami asked excitedly.

"While you can do your room in every shade of pink imaginable, I would prefer another color for the kitchen. Fair?" Jan asked.

"Definitely fair," Ami declared with a giggle. They both laughed.

Chapter 3

Ami stood thoughtfully in front of the paint chips at Sam's. She had already put a couple aside for her room--hint of pink, pink rose and light gray. Those she had picked while comparing swatches of material she carried with her. She was excited about that because Jan had never let her choose her own colors before, and her room had always been a neutral tone like ivory or white. She was also really excited about her brand-new furniture and linens.

But the task of the day was the kitchen. What color should she choose? She walked over to the fall shades. The kitchen had previously been decorated in a fall scheme and Ami felt that it was right to keep to that. But she didn't want to just paint the walls. The cabinets were rather boring now and she had an idea to liven them up. She picked a light golden brown for the wall color. Then for the cabinet doors she intended to paint them in color blocks. Above the counter, the cabinets themselves were going to be a light burgundy. The doors would be a light sage. But below the counter a darker burgundy would be used for the cabinet and a dark sage would be used on the doors.

She showed her selections to Jan, who looked at them really hard as if trying to imagine it.

"I do like it, but I think we'd be better with just the lighter colors all around."

Ami nodded. "All right." She tried to keep the sound of disappointment out of her voice.

He grinned. "I think yours would look great. I just don't really want to deal with that many colors of paint, if the truth were told. The brushes would be a pain to clean. Plus I would have to be organized about painting the doors." He thought a moment. "What would you say to that golden brown being the main color we used in the house. I really like it."

"Sounds like a plan!"

"We'll go ahead and get the paint now, including the ones for your room. We're really ahead of schedule, thanks to your great work in the kitchen."

"What's left?" Ami asked.

"Hmm...Fortunately, the plumbing and electrical all checked out perfectly, but we still have to wash the walls in all the rooms but the living room. Then we'll paint. Once that's done, we are going to strip the floors." He smiled at her. "I was thinking of driving you over to Mill's Valley tomorrow, to the mall, after the floors are stripped. You need to get some new outfits for school this year. And some supplies, I'm sure. If you will spare me the torment of shopping, I'll spare you the torment of refinishing the floors. How does that sound to you? "

Ami was shocked. "Shopping...by myself?"

"If you wouldn't mind?"

"Mind? No, I'm really looking forward to it."

"The moving van should arrive the day after, and then we'll have to unpack and organize. But I think we'll have everything ready before classes start, and the plant is ready to start hiring," Jan said, confidently.

Ami nodded. She actually was enjoying bringing the beauty back into the lonely, old house. She could already feel it becoming more like home. Maybe Jan had been on to something about renovating their home. After Jan paid for all of the supplies, they headed back to the house to put them in the hallway. It was late and they were pretty much finished for the day. As they prepared to head back to the hotel, Ami grabbed her bag of stuff and put her Walkman back into it. "Is there a bookstore in town, Dad?" she asked.

"I don't know. Why don't we explore a bit before we head back to the hotel? It would be nice to know a little more about the town we're making our home."

Ami nodded. She walked with Jan over to the Plymouth Caravelle that he drove. It was a pretty blue car, and ran nicely. "Would you like to drive?"

"Would I!" Ami exclaimed as she took the keys from Jan before he could change his mind. She settled in the car and ran through all of the checks she needed to do, especially with Jan in the car. With the move, she had not been able to get her own car.

She took it slowly driving down the lane to the main street. Ami drove into the town center and she parked the car. "I figured we could walk around."

The majority of the stores were located in this central location on Main Street. There were a few, like Sam's Hardware and Sew Right, which were located in more rural areas. And there was another area out by the hotel, about three miles from town center, where another commercial center was located. Here in town center, at the beginning of Main Street, was the local Piggly Wiggly. Opposite that was Taylor's Falls Credit Union. There was a pizza parlor/bowling alley, which was where Jan had come earlier for their pizza. Ami noticed a 'Help Wanted' sign. This was not the time for her to apply for a job--she wanted to wait until school started so she could get a feel for her schedule, and how hard the classes were here, before committing to that. They had a used book store, and a video rental store. There was a little sandwich shop and a restaurant of some kind. Taylor's Falls had an independent department store that seemed to sell a little of everything. Of course, there was a Ben Franklin's Five and Dime, and a Salvation Army Thrift Store. The post office and City Hall were also in this small stretch of stores. An antiques store rounded out the area.

Out by the hotel they had a few other things, like McDonald's, another grocery store, Shoney's Restaurant and Pizza Hut. Ami was pretty tired of Shoney's breakfast right now, and was looking forward to a home cooked meal.

To be honest, there really was not much here.

Ami could see construction on a movie theater being done a little farther down. It looked like it was going to feature double screens. But for now, if she wanted to see a movie, she'd have to drive out to Mill's Valley Mall.

That was okay. When their stuff arrived, Ami had a television set and VCR for her room. She owned a few movies, but the video rental store would be a place she'd use.

The town would probably build up soon with the manufacturing plant that was going to open here. That was why they had moved here. Her father, Jan, had been transferred to manage this new facility.

"Oh look, Central High's colors are Blue and Red," Ami said. "And it looks like their mascot is a lion."

Jan smiled. "We probably should show a little spirit and go get shirts, huh?"

Ami nodded. She wanted to join the cheerleading squad, so showing spirit was very important. "That would be great. And I would like to look in the book store. I'm almost finished with the books I brought with me."

"All right. We'll go to the department store and get shirts, then split up. I'm going to go look and see if there are any antiques that would look good in the house. I'll come find you if I finish first--or you can come find me if I take too long."

The pair went into the department store and Ami was excited to find a powder blue and pink t-shirt that said "Central Lions" on it, since pink was her favorite color. Jan picked out a more standard blue and red shirt for himself. Ami headed over to the bookstore, determined to find at least one new novel to read.

She smiled as she entered the used book store. It smelled right--just that hint of musk and paper. It was also a nice cozy store, with a few chairs scattered around. Right now, no one was taking advantage of the chairs. Ami walked around the store to get a feel for what kind of books they had. When she turned the corner to the sci-fi section, she was surprised to find a calico cat sitting on one of the book stools. "Well, hello sweetie. What's your name?" she asked as she approached the cat.

"Mrrrph" the cat chirred. Ami bent down and scratched her head. She looked for a collar, which she hoped would have a name tag. "There we go. I see you're called Chessie. Well, that's a pretty name. Pleased to meet you, Chessie. Do you have anything you'd like to recommend?"

Chessie blinked at her, then rubbed up against a book. Why not? Ami thought. She picked it up and decided to go ahead and get Chessie's 'recommendation.'

"I see you've made a friend, Chessie. Would you care to introduce us?" Ami looked down the aisle and saw an older woman walking towards them. Chessie hopped down and rubbed up against the woman's legs. "Hi, I'm Annabelle Lee."

"Amilou Polowski. But I go by Ami." She smiled, and forced herself not to throw in a Poe quote.

Annabelle smiled. "In case you're wondering, no, my parents didn't do that to me. I was born Annabelle Jones and married Chad Lee. Thus, Annabelle Lee." As Ami looked at her again, she realized that Annabelle wasn't really that old – it was just something about her style of dress. She dressed in clothes that were very out of style, according to the magazines, but somehow completely perfectly fit her personality. The material itself was faded purple washing into a faded teal, with an intricate pattern drawn out in burnished gold all throughout the fabric. The edge of the floor length dress was embroidered and had little tiny bells sewn around the bottom, so Ami could hear Annabelle's movement. The belt was a dark purple macramé style, with butterflies worked into the design. It was actually quite a charming outfit, and Ami envied Annabelle her confidence to wear something so totally unusual and totally fitting her personality.

"I have always thought that had a pretty ring to it," Ami commented. "The poem's very sad, but I loved the name."

"Me, too, and I figured I'd go with it. That's why I named the shop 'The Kingdom by the Sea'." Annabelle said with a grin.

Ami smiled. "I had wondered about that. It seemed an odd name for a book shop, but now it makes perfect sense!"

"Are you new in town or just here visiting? I see you have a 'Chessie Recommendation'."

"Does she do that a lot?"

Annabelle nodded. "It's her thing. You'll probably love it. Most people do."

"Good! Well, my dad and I just moved here. He's going to oversee the plant."

Annabelle nodded. "We are all hoping that this plant will help the area. So, have you found a place yet?"

"Just up the road a bit. It's an older white house up on the hill that we're in the process of cleaning up. It's apparently been vacant for a long time," Ami said. "But it really is a gorgeous house. I can't understand why no one has bought it."

Annabelle tilted her head back a moment and looked like she was considering whether or not to say anything. Then she nodded and shrugged. "It's just local superstition, of course, but some say that house is cursed."

"Cursed?"   Ami was shocked.

"It's just local silliness," Annabelle said with a small laugh. "But they say that because the couple who bought it last stayed there only one night. The wife died that evening when she was sleepwalking in the yard."

"That's awful," Ami said.

"It was. Her husband never really got over it, the poor dear."

Ami was not sure what to say.

"Come along, I'll give you the grand tour of my little kingdom," Annabelle offered.

The next morning, after yet another breakfast at Shoney's, Ami and Jan headed over to the house for a day of work. Jan started working on the rest of the walls, while Ami tackled the kitchen. She took all the doors off the cabinets, and took them outside. She spread a tarp on the grass and painted one side of the doors. Then she went back inside and she painted the cabinets themselves. She put on her Walkman to listen to music, but with Jan in the house, she only hummed along. She decided to check and see if the doors were dry enough to flip over while the cabinets were drying. She was hoping to get as much done in the kitchen today as possible, so that she could start on her room soon.

The doors were indeed ready to be turned over, so she was able to paint the other side.

"Ami, I heard it was going to rain!" Jan called from the door. Ami had not seen any clouds, so she was a bit surprised by Jan's warning. He walked over. "Let me help you get these on the porch so they don't get watered down, if it does."

"I hope it doesn't rain, Dad," Ami said. "Paint dries faster when it's dry outside."

He smiled. "Yes, it does. Glad I caught you before you started this side. These would have been a pain to move with wet paint."

Ami nodded in agreement, raising her eyebrows as she realized how annoying it would have been.

They got all the doors laid out on the porch when the first rain cloud showed up. "On second thought," Jan said. "Let's move these inside. If they are on the tarp, you can still paint them in here, especially since the floors haven't been done yet."

They set the last of the doors inside and shut the front door when the rain started pounding into the grass. "That was just weird!" Ami exclaimed. "I mean, you just said it, and now it's raining."

Jan nodded.

Ami and Jan walked through the house. The movers would be here in the morning with their things. Appliances had been installed yesterday, as had the telephone. First up was the kitchen. Ami smiled as she looked at it. This room she had done by herself. She had stripped wallpaper, picked paint, painted and hung racks for their pans.

Jan congratulated her. "Came out real nice. I think Sofia would have liked this room a lot. Good job."

"Thanks, Dad."

Next they walked into the living room. The newly finished floors shone, and the wall color was very rich and inviting. They had had the extra time to build an entertainment center/book shelf wall unit. The wall unit was painted in a slightly darker shade of golden brown, and looked great in the room. Of course, Jan had an extensive collection of books which would soon be loaded in it, which would make it even more amazing. They had left a space in the center for a painting that Sofia, Ami's mother, had painted of the view outside their last home. She had finished it only a month before she died and they had never really found a place for it before. This would showcase it. Jan had even installed a frame light above where it would hang.

"I like this room, Dad," Ami said.

"Me, too."

The bathrooms were very neutral, chosen that way so that they could accessorize them however they felt, whenever they felt like changing the style.

The dining room chandelier had been soaked and cleaned. It shimmered. They had painted this room in the darker golden brown, matching the book units.

Jan's bedroom was very neutrally prepared. But Ami loved her room.

She had painted the walls a soft pink, so soft it was almost white. Her built in book unit was made to be the frame of her bed. It had a reading light built into it, and it had been painted rose. The baseboards were painted gray, and Ami had painted a border of gray and pink swirls around the top of the room.

"You really worked hard on this one, didn't you?" Jan asked as he stared at the border.

Ami nodded.

"I think you got some of your mother's artistic ability. That boarder is beautiful."

"Thanks!"

"Well, early start tomorrow. Why don't we head over to El Burro for dinner?"

"That sounds great." Ami agreed readily. It was not quite as good as the Mexican restaurants in Santa Fe, but it was still very good. El Burro was quickly becoming Ami's favorite restaurant in town, although she missed Taco Bell and Chinese food. Still, with the plant coming, maybe those would come to Taylor's Falls soon, too.

The day did start early. They finally checked out of the hotel, because tonight, they'd be sleeping at their new home.

Ami didn't remember them having packed so much stuff, but clearly they did. She helped Jan direct boxes and pieces of furniture. The movers arrived, as promised, at 7:30 a.m. And they unloaded the truck until about 11:00 a.m. From that time, Jan and Ami worked on the house. They got the beds set up first, so that when they were exhausted, at least they'd have somewhere to sleep. Then Ami headed to the kitchen and Jan headed to the living room.

While Ami was unpacking boxes, she was talking to herself. The first thing she noticed was how dirty the plates had gotten while wrapped in newspaper.

So everything had to be cleaned. She loaded as much as she could in the dishwasher, then ran it. While the dishwasher was running, Ami washed pans and put them in the cabinets nearest the stove. The counter nearest the stove was also the longest of the counters, so she decided that would be where most of the cooking and baking would be done. There she put the baking items and the storage containers. As soon as the dishwasher finished, she put the dishes up above it. Glasses went nearest the refrigerator.

She was very glad to see extra cabinet space was available. Next was to figure out where to put the toaster, mixer and microwave. The microwave she placed near the refrigerator. Toaster and mixer went near the stove.

Jan walked in, looking pretty beat. "Living room is unpacked.   Want to see it?"

"Sure," Ami said, needing a break herself. "We probably should go to the grocery store--at least get some things for breakfast."

She looked in at the living room. The bookcase was almost completely full, as she had expected it would be. The television was set up, as was the VCR. And Mom's picture looked beautiful where it was hung. "I like it."

"Me, too. Let's go get those groceries."

By the time they got back from the grocery store and put all the groceries away, Ami was exhausted. She had hoped to at least get a start on her room tonight. The other rooms wouldn't take nearly as long as the kitchen. And she didn't expect to have everything done tonight. But it would have been nice to have at least unpacked one box.

She decided to wait until the morning though. Ami took a shower, dried her hair out, and then went to bed.

In Ami's dream, she unpacked her boxes. She seemed to move effortlessly from one box to the next, and as she finished with a box, it disappeared from the room. She set her book collection in the four shelves to her right, and her stuffed animals in the cubbies above her bed. Her white desk was set up with her school supplies. Pictures of her friends were displayed in the corkboard frame they had given her. She set up her television stand and got her VCR hooked up. She had her clothes all folded or hung up, and where they belonged. All of her knic knacs had found a cute home. It was perfect. Ami had even found the window swing seat that she had wanted, but that Jan had told her she couldn't have. It went up very easily and turned out to be much sturdier than she expected it would be.

Ami found a few things she thought she'd loaned to other people, and had not been able to get back. She found a place for all those things. She looked at her room. It was absolutely perfect. Everything matched perfectly. All of the clothes in her wardrobe, except her cheer uniform from Memorial HS and her powder blue and pink shirt for Central, were either pink, white, or gray. She didn't remember her clothes matching so well before, but they went perfectly with her perfect room.

Ami groaned as the sun light burst into the room. She was not looking forward to unpacking today, and while she was looking forward to having her room done--she didn't actually relish putting it together.

When she opened her eyes, though, she was completely baffled.

Her room was done--and it looked exactly like it had in her dream. Had she done this in her sleep?

Chapter 4

Ami had seen a few other teenagers around town, but she'd always been with her dad as they were buying supplies for the renovation, and she didn't want to make Jan work on the house alone. They had finished the house ahead of schedule and actually had time to work on her tree house. Aside from a few railings that needed repairs, the tree house was in great shape. So she painted the inside walls while Jan repaired the damaged rails. Jan paid someone to come and run a power line to the tree house. They put a lock on the door, and Ami found a boom box, small television and VCR at the thrift shop. Those went into the hideaway, along with cushions. Jan surprised her with a mini fridge and a microwave. "So you can make popcorn and keep some drinks up here. But I better not find alcohol. Or boys," he added as an afterthought. "Understood?"

Ami grinned. "Absolutely."

"So, what do you think?" Jan asked her.

"I love it!" Ami could already see that she would be spending nearly as much time here as in her room, especially if she could make some friends. It would be a great place for them to hang out, where they could talk without disturbing her father.

The next day, school would be starting. Ami was more than a little nervous at the prospect. She had lived in Santa Fe her whole life, so the first day of school always meant seeing friends again, and making new ones. Today, she would be a complete outsider, and she only hoped that a few kind souls would take pity on her.

In the morning, Ami and Jan walked out to the car so he could drive her to school. "How about you drive?" He handed her a set of keys on a pink key chain, obviously chosen for her. Her very own set of keys to the car! Ami was more than thrilled at the trust Jan was giving her. "You can drop me off at the hardware store. It's pretty close to the school. I'll come get the car when I'm done."

Ami gave him a hug. "Thanks, Dad."

"I expect you'll be taking the bus home, but I figured it wouldn't hurt to drive the first day."

She nodded and got behind the wheel. Jan was being very cool. Letting her drive to school might not earn her any cool points, but she would definitely lose them if she got out of a car driven by her dad.

Ami dropped Jan off at the hardware store, and saw him cross over to the restaurant which was open for breakfast. She laughed. He'd probably be having a big cup of coffee and a muffin as soon as he got there. She turned back onto the street and drove to Taylor's Falls Central High School, or, as everyone around here called it, "Central." There were only a few other cars in the parking lot, so finding a space was not too difficult. She parked the car, took her book bag out, and locked the car. Then she slowly walked toward the building.

Jan had picked her schedule up yesterday, so she knew what rooms all of her classes were in; however, she was not sure where everything was. She looked at her schedule again, hoping to be able to figure out where to go.

Ami was looking down at her schedule when she saw a pair of pink shoes stop in front of her.

"Hi. You're new. What's your name? I'm Jennie, Jennie Jennison. Bad I know." Jennie had dark blonde hair, which was pulled back in a ponytail, and hazel eyes. She also had a very friendly smile.

"Ami Polowski," Ami responded.

"I'm glad to meet you. Welcome to Central. So, who do you have for home room?"

Ami looked down again. "Ms. Carter."

Jennie grinned. "Great! So do I. I'll walk with you. Did you get your locker assignment? I know we don't have a lot of books yet, but trust me, by the end of today, you are going to want to know where it is."

Ami was shocked. Jennie was very friendly, and talked quickly. She nodded. "Um. 104B."

"Great!" Jennie said as she waved to a couple of other girls.   "You're really close to mine. They're right on the way, so I'll show you on our way to class." She paused. "That's Bobbi Jones and Lyn Andrews," Jennie commented as the other girls started to walk towards them. Bobbi was a brunette, with a very chic bob. She dressed very preppy. Lyn had red, medium length hair and a lot of freckles. She wore jeans and Central t-shirt.

Ami was thrilled. It seemed that Jennie was one of those people who took on strays, and Ami was definitely a stray. Bobbi and Lyn seemed like totally different people, but it didn't seem to matter to Jennie. She greeted them both warmly.

"Bobbi, Lyn, this is Ami Polowski. She's in our home room," Jennie said. "She just moved here."

Bobbi smiled and nodded at her. Lyn looked to Jennie then back to Ami. "Welcome to Central."

The four girls walked towards their class, with Jennie introducing people as they walked past. Jennie was really nice though. She might say, "Oh, that's Sue. She's really a sweet girl." But she never said "That's Derrik.   You'll want to stay away from him." She didn't talk negatively about any of the kids they passed by. All the while, Jennie was peppering Ami with questions. By the time they got to home room, Jennie already knew that Ami was a junior from Santa Fe who had been on the cheerleading squad and liked to do theatre. And Ami knew that Jennie was also a cheerleader, Lyn was a dancer, and Bobbi wanted to be a writer. Ami knew that she really liked all of these girls.

While they were waiting for home room to start, Jennie looked at Ami's schedule and drew up a map of where she needed to go and how to get there. Jennie had also seemed really pleased when she found out they had the same lunch period. Ami was probably more pleased, because it meant she'd see at least one friendly face during that time. Jennie also dispensed a lot of advice about the school so Ami could be better prepared. "Oh, and watch out for Dr. Thomas. He doesn't like it when you're late. Always prepare for his class, because he will call on you. If you don't understand it, he's cool. But if you didn't try, he gets really testy and assigns everyone extra problems."

"Good to know. That's one way to make people hate me before I get a chance here."

Jennie laughed. "Did you want to try out for the cheerleading team here? Tryouts are today."

Ami paled. "I forgot to work out a routine." How could she have been so stupid!

"Oh, just do a few from your school. I'm sure they're pretty similar, and you know that once you start one of those, it's almost automatic."

The bell rang. Ordinarily, homeroom was a bit of a waste of time. Basically, attendance was taken. Announcements were made. Allegiance was pledged. Basic stuff. Then they dispersed to their classes. But for Ami today, it had been very helpful. On the way out, Jennie stopped Ami. "I'll meet you at your locker for lunch, if that's all right. Bobbi and Lyn don't have the same lunch, but you'll get to meet Patty."

It seemed that Jennie had just adopted Ami into her circle of friends. "That would be great." Ami was excited to not have to look for Jennie, or feel like she was imposing.

"I hope you don't think I'm a pest," Jennie started.

"No. You're a lifesaver. I probably would have spent the next three days working up the nerve to talk to people." Ami smiled.

"Been there." Jennie laughed. "I am a pretty good judge of people and you looked like someone I'd get along really well with, and I was the new kid about three years ago. Took me a week and a half."

Ami grinned. "See you at lunch!"

By lunchtime, Ami already had three books to store in her locker. True to her word, Jennie was waiting for Ami at her locker. She was standing next to another girl. This girl had short black hair and wore a black linen skirt and white top. "Hi Jennie."

"Hey Ami. This is Patty."

Patty waved shyly and Ami smiled at her.

"So, how're classes going so far?"

"Not too bad," Ami said. "So far, I like all my teachers."

"You're lucky," Patty said.

Jennie gave Patty a hug. "You'll find that a lot of people tend to shy away from Patty. So, let's just get this over with."

Here it was. A test.

Patty looked at Ami. "I'm psychic. It freaks people out."

"Why would that freak them out? I mean, unless you're walking up to someone and saying 'you're going to die on November 18 next year,' it doesn't seem like it should matter. Right?"

Patty laughed. "You're absolutely right. And I don't. But I do have a little reputation for saying odd things."

Ami grinned. "If you're trying to scare me off, you're failing miserably. I think that sounds fascinating!"

Patty visibly relaxed. "You really mean that." She sounded shocked.

"Course I do!" Ami said.

Jennie smiled. "Great, now that's settled. Let's go see what kind of garbage they are serving today." She looked at Ami. "You're probably going to want to pack your lunch most days. First day of school is usually pretty good, but if you see meatloaf on the menu, don't trust it. We're juniors this year, so if we have our parents' permission, we can leave campus during lunch."

"You walk to town for lunch?"

"No. I have a car. So you and Patty can ride with me," Jennie said.

The three walked over to the cafeteria. Ami was starting to get a feel for this school. It had the same cliques as Memorial had. There were the Burn Outs, the Nerds, the Popular girls, the Jocks, music freaks, and the unclassified. The cafeteria had almost the same layout. And the food even smelled the same.

"So, where do you live?" Jennie asked as they sat down at an unoccupied table.

"Oh, that old white house about a mile out of town. On a little hill."

Patty looked at her. "You mean the old Miller place?"

Ami shrugged. "I don't know. It has a gorgeous two story tree house."

Jennie nodded. "The Miller place. It's cursed."

Patty agreed. "It is."

"It's really nice," Ami insisted. "Of course, Annabelle Lee down at the bookstore also mentioned a curse, but she didn't tell me what that curse was."

"No one knows. We just know it is," Jennie said.

"Have you ever been out there?" Ami asked.

They both shook their heads to indicate they had not. But it was obvious that they both very much wanted to.

"You're welcome to come by. I'm sure Dad wouldn't mind," Ami offered.

Jennie looked down. "Do you mind if I ask you a personal question?"

Ami shrugged. "Sure."

"You keep mentioning your dad. But where's your mom? Did they get divorced or something?"

"No. Mom died a couple years ago." Ami didn't give further details and Jennie didn't ask.

"I'm sorry," Jennie said softly.

"Me too," Patty said. "Unfortunately, it means we have something in common."

"You lost your mom too? I'm sorry."

"I actually don't have parents. I live out in the 'children's home.' Actually, it's the 'William T and

Julia Emma Carlisle Home For Children,' and everyone calls it the 'children's home' since it's easier to say. I just wish they'd at least give it a less demeaning name."

"Wow." Ami had no way to respond to that. She shrugged. "We could always just refer to it as 'Bill's Place'," Ami offered.

Patty grinned. "I doubt that would catch on. People who don't live there don't really care. But I do have great friends who are almost like a family, right Jennie?"

"You got it, sis!"

Ami laughed. She missed having friends that close. But it seemed like she was well on her way to making some new ones already.

Ami followed Jennie to the gymnasium after classes were over for the day. Jennie had been on the squad last year, but was also required to try out again this year. The only person who didn't have to was Cindy Holcombe, the squad leader. She had been the top junior last year.

Ami signed up for tryouts, right under Jennie. She was rather glad she was not the first to go--she would be able to get a feel for what this team's spirit was about. She didn't know if they were more acrobatic or more dance oriented. If it was an acrobatic squad, Ami wouldn't be able to turn a good audition. However, she was fairly confident of any dance routines. Those routines were more fun to do, and much less dangerous.

Ami noticed that most of the girls had brought their own tapes, with songs they had choreographed. "Oh no," Ami whispered.

"What?" Jennie asked.

"I don't have any routine music." She did have her Walkman with her; however, she didn't have copies of the music they used.

"Just a moment." Jennie dug in her bag and pulled out a tape. The case was labeled with all of the songs on it. "Know a routine to any of these?"

Ami looked at the tape. "Lucky Star. We did one to that."

"Great. I'll let you use it after I'm done. You have your Walkman, right?"

Ami nodded.

"Then just set it up once I give it to you. Lucky Star is number seven. I'm doing number three."

"Jennie. I can't thank you enough."

"It's what friends do," Jennie said.

"Well, I'm certainly glad you decided to be my friend this morning," Ami said.

"It was mutual, I think," Jennie said.

Ami and Jennie watched all of the girls audition. When Jennie's turn came up, Ami frowned. Jennie was not doing well. She'd obviously tried to choreograph the routine herself, and it was not working. She knew how to move, but her choreography was atrocious. Hopefully the coach would see the skill set, not the order of moves. Of course, Jennie had been on the squad last year, so the coach did have something else to use as a judge. Besides, Jennie was using music they had done routines for here, and she obviously couldn't do their routine.

But Ami also felt it would be awful if she made the team and Jennie didn't.

She queued up "Lucky Star." Because they had not seen the Memorial HS routine, Ami didn't have to try to design one. She just did the routine they did to it. From Jennie's reaction, she could tell she had done pretty good.

After the last girl had tried out on individual routines, the coach had everyone come onto the field and taught them a cheer which they had to perform. Ami and Jennie both picked up the routine quickly, and Ami was relieved to see that.

Finally, the tryout was over. "Thank you all for coming out today," Coach Grant said. "I'll have the team roster posted tomorrow morning on the gym door. If you make the squad, come in and get your uniform and gear. Practice will start Wednesday. Any questions?"

There were none, so Jennie and Ami left. "What time is your dad expecting you home?" Jennie asked.

"Soon. Why?"

"Bobbi, Lyn, Patty and I usually would do something after we all get done. I wanted to know if you wanted to come, too."

Ami nodded. "I would. But I really should check with my dad."

"All right. We're going to be at my house. Let me give you my number. You can call once you get to talk to your dad. Your phone is connected, right?"

"Yeah."

Jennie wrote down her number. "When you call, I'll give you directions to my place. Or depending on what we decide to do, we might come pick you up."

"All right."

They went to their lockers to get their books, then walked down to the parking lot. Ami was surprised to see that Jan's car was still in the parking lot. She smiled. He must have decided to let her drive home as well. She waved goodbye to Jennie and walked over to the car.

Chapter 5

As Ami drove home, she reflected on her day. Classes didn't seem too bad. The teachers were nice. The cheerleading tryout had gone well. And she had four friends already. It had been a great day.

Ami drove into town first, just to see if Jan was hanging around any of the stores and needing a ride home. Sure enough, he was sitting out front of the bookstore. Ami pulled up.

"Cheer tryouts?"

Ami nodded.

"How did you do?"

"I'll find out tomorrow. I think I did good though. And I met some really nice girls."

Jan smiled. "Great. Why don't you tell me about them on the way home?"

Ami nodded. "Well, Jennie Jennison, she's the really outgoing one who introduced me to the others, she also tried out for the cheerleading squad. She's in my homeroom with me. She, Bobbi Jones, and Lyn Andrews are all in my homeroom. The other girl is Patty. I don't remember her last name. But anyway, they're all meeting at Jennie's house tonight. And Jennie invited me over too. If it's all right with you, of course."

"I think it might be. But I would like to meet them. Why don't you invite them for dinner, if it's not too late?"

"That would be great, Dad. I'll call Jennie when we get home and see if they can come for dinner."

Ami pulled up to their house and parked the car. Jan headed to the house while Ami grabbed her book bag. She came inside and set the bag on the table. Then she called Jennie.

"Jennie. This is Ami, from school."

Jennie laughed. "I remember you Ami. So, what did your dad say?"

"He wants to meet all of you, and suggested you come over for dinner," Ami said. "It's okay if you don't want to."

She heard Lyn in the background "I want to see your house!"

The sentiment was echoed by all of the girls.

"Let me check with my mom. Hold on." Jennie set down the phone and Bobbi picked up.

"So, how did you like your first day here at Central?" Bobbi asked.

"I liked it a lot, actually. I was thinking I'd be a lot more homesick, but I'm not."

"Good. Look, if Jennie's mom says she can't, don't take it personally. Her parents are really strict. They may want to meet your parents before they'll let her come over for dinner. That's why we hang out over here so much--it's easier."

Ami didn't know what to say. "Okay."

"Jennie doesn't mention it much, and I know she'll be disappointed."

"Well, the truth is, my dad wants to meet you guys before he lets me hang out alone with you, too, so I can completely understand. We'll see what her parents say, and then see what we can work out."

"Oh, another one with strict parents, huh?" Lyn said in the background.

"Parent," Patty said softly.

"What?" Lyn asked

"Bobbi, would you ask Ami if she minds if I tell you?" Patty asked.

Ami heard her. "Tell Patty it would be a lot easier on me if she would. I don't like to talk about it, but you guys deserve to know."

"All right," Bobbi said, sounding confused. She relayed to Patty.

Jennie came back. "Mom says she wants to meet your dad first, Ami. Think he could swing by?"

"Let me go ask. I'll be right back."

Ami went to the living room. "Dad? Mrs. Jenison wants to meet you before Jennie can come over for dinner."

"Then I'll drive over with you. I would like to meet them too."

"Great!"

She went back to the phone. "My dad is going to come over with me."

"Super! We'll figure out the plan after our parents get a chance to meet each other and decide that we're all okay." Jennie laughed.

Mrs. Elaine Jenison answered the door and welcome Ami and Jan into the house. "The girls are upstairs, dear. First door on the left."

"Thanks, Mrs. Jenison," Ami said. She looked at Jan, who waved her on. Two younger kids came up to her.

"I'm Carrie." "I'm Jamie." The girl and boy spoke almost in unison.

"You're new," Carrie said. "Do you go to school with Jennie?"

"Yes. I just moved here. I'm Ami."

"Are you a cheerleader?   You look like a cheerleader," Jamie said.

Ami shrugged. "I hope to be. I tried out with Jennie today."

"Did you see Jennie's car? She likes to drive really fast, but Mom and Dad don't know that because she's never been caught by the cops. But she will be some time, I know." Jamie paused to take a breath as they reached Jennie's door.

Jennie came out and gave the two a look. "I see you have met my younger pests--I mean, brother and sister."

Ami nodded. "I wish I had a brother or a sister."

"Wanna take one home with you?"

"Jennie!" Carrie shouted.

"Kidding squirt," the older sister said, ruffling Carrie's hair.

"Come on in, Ami. Everyone's here."

Elaine offered Jan a glass of tea. "I'm Elaine and this is my husband, Dennis."

"Jan Polowski."

"What do you do, Mr. Polowski," Jane asked.

"Oh, please call me Jan. I'm the manager of operations over at the plant over on Highway 27."

Dennis nodded. "Great for the area, I can tell you. We have all been very excited to hear about this chip factory. There really haven't been a lot of opportunities here for kids. Many of them leave after college, because they don't want to work for the Piggly Wiggly. It's going to mean a lot more people in the area, and traffic here, too."

"I can certainly understand. We're taking applications starting Monday, so if you know anyone who is interested, please tell them to come by the plant."

Dennis nodded. "What kinds of positions are available?"

"Supervisors, line workers, drivers, mechanics, office staff. We're looking to almost fully staff the factory with people from here. It will be a few weeks before the plant opens, and we hope to have most of our associates in place by that time. Dennis, what line of work are you in?"

"I'm an accountant. Mostly self-employed, but I was thinking about going to work in the corporate world. Would you be hiring any accountants?"

Jan nodded. "Definitely. We want to keep the plant records accurate."

"Then I will be sure to see you on Monday."

"Why don't you let Ami stay for dinner with us today?" Elaine said. "She seems like a charming young lady, what I did see of her before she went upstairs. Dennis will be more than happy to drive her home when he takes the other girls home tonight."

"Do they spend a lot of time here?"

"Oh yes. Patty is an orphan, the poor thing. Lyn's parents are barely home. And since Bobby is also close to both of the other girls, she's here a lot too. They do their homework together. We like to make sure Jennie's gets done, and if we're checking hers, we figure we might as well keep up with the other girls. I'm home all day," Elaine said. "So you're more than welcome to have Ami come here after school with Jennie. That way she doesn't have to go home to an empty house."

"How late do they generally stay?" Jan asked.

Dennis responded. "On school nights, I take them home at 8:30. Most of the girls are in sports, so they don't come over on Friday nights--since there is a game. But Saturdays they have slumber parties. They tend to rotate that from house to house."

"Sounds like my little girl really did okay for herself then on the first day of school." Jan said seriously.

"I think they'll welcome her just fine into their circle. They do often go to Mill's Valley Mall, but that's only on Saturdays, and not every week either. I think they like to go to movies once in a while. Jennie usually drives. But that's just because she's the only one with a car."

Jan nodded. He approved of Jennie's parents and felt comfortable with Ami visiting over here. It also alleviated one of his worries. He didn't like the idea of her coming home to an empty house during the week. He knew that shortly, his hours would be very long, and he wouldn't be getting home from work before 7 p.m. nightly. If Ami had a place to be, he knew she'd be safe.

"I have to say, I'm really grateful for you having Ami over here.   Please don't be insulted by my offer. You're going to be feeding my daughter several days a week. I really feel like I should be helping with the grocery bill."

Dennis laughed. "That's not necessary. But I can't say I don't appreciate the offer. If we were doing this for boys, you can bet I'd take you up on it. Usually the girls all help Elaine with the cooking and clean up."

"Wonderful. Ami hasn't had much training in cooking since Sofia--" He stopped to gather his thoughts again. "Since Sofia's death. I'm no good in the kitchen."

"Elaine is a wonderful cook, I don't mind bragging. Tell ya what, why don't you stay for dinner, too?"

"A home cooked meal? Oh, I'm not going to turn that down."

Ami sat down on Jennie's floor. They all had their books out and were working on homework. "Anyone good at math?"

"That would be me," Bobbi said. "Geometry, right?"

Ami nodded.

"Let's have a look, then." Bobbi looked over the problems that Ami was working on and talked her through fairly easily.

"Ami, what's your best subject?"

"I'm pretty good with science and history."

"Great. Lyn is good with science, too. And Jennie's our grammar maven. Patty is great with literature. We've always had issues with history, so now we have everything."

"Cool." Ami had not just found a group of friends, she'd also found a study group.

Patty stood looking at the tapes. "What should we listen to? George, INXS, Guns & Roses or Gloria?"

"INXS," Lyn said.

Patty popped in the cassette. Ami and Bobbi worked a bit more on her math. Then they started on their English reading assignment. Finally, they were all finished with homework.

Jennie, Lyn, Bobbi and Patty stood up. "Time to go help mom with dinner," Jennie said.

Ami nodded and followed them downstairs. She was a bit surprised to see her dad still there, visiting with Mr. and Mrs. Jenison. Jan stayed in the living room with Dennis Jenison as the women went into the kitchen.

Elaine got the ingredients out for dinner. "Ami, hope you don't mind helping."

"No, Mrs. Jenison. Not at all." Ami said. She waited for instructions. Elaine set Lyn and Bobbi on mashed potatoes. Patty was fixing a quick dessert.

Jennie was working with her mom on the fried chicken. And Ami had been assigned the salad.

She listened happily as the girls all told Mrs. Jenison about their days. Ami realized that Mrs. Jenison was very much like a mother to Patty, in particular, who had no mother of her own. She swallowed an uncomfortable lump in her throat, determined not to get emotional.

Mrs. Jenison patted her on the shoulder.

Ami watched Jennie and Mrs. Jenison make the fried chicken. All of the girls gathered around as it fried.

"How do you know when it's done, Mrs. J?" Bobbi asked.

Mrs. Jenison picked up a fork and stabbed one of the pieces. "See that? The juice is clear. That means this piece is done. If its reddish or pink, it needs a little more time." She removed the tested piece of chicken and dried it off, then placed it in a basket. All of the chicken was soon finished.

"I don't think I have ever had fried chicken that didn't come from KFC," Ami said.

"Then you are in for a treat, my dear. This is my grandmother's secret recipe. And someday, I might share it with all of you. Might," Mrs. Jenison said, with a grin.

They set the table, and the others all joined them. Jan had been playing Scrabble with Dennis, Carrie and Jamie.

"This smells delicious, dear," Dennis said, giving his wife a kiss on the cheek. They passed around the food, as everyone took a moment to talk about their day.

Jan was extremely glad he had decided to let Ami stay for dinner this evening. It was one of the best meals he had eaten in a very long time, and not just because the food was so wonderful.

This was a great environment for Ami to spend her evenings. He was very proud of her. She had picked amazing friends--or rather, amazing friends had picked her. True, he had just met them; however, sometimes, it didn't take long before you got a good feel for someone. He could already tell that Dennis would be a great employee. He thought he would be just the right person to manage the accounting department.

True, he had not conducted a formal interview; however, this informal evening had told him even more about his future employee than an interview could. He was honest. He valued family. This was the atmosphere he wanted to foster at the plant. Of course, Dennis would have to be properly vetted through human resources; however, as long as everything checked out, this was one of his hiring decisions finished.

"So, who is hosting the slumber party this weekend?" Elaine asked.

Ami looked at Jan. "Could we have it at my house? I mean, if it's okay with my dad, of course."

The other girls all chattered excitedly. "That would be great." "Oh, sounds like fun." "Cool!"

Jan frowned. "I don't know. I actually have a business trip this weekend. I'm not going to be home. Elaine, Dennis, how would you feel about that?"

Elaine frowned a few moments. "I think we should go talk this over in the kitchen." Elaine, Dennis, and Jan got up and went into the kitchen.

"Do you think they'll agree?" Lyn asked. Her parents wouldn't care, but if Jennie couldn't come, it wouldn't be fair.

"I don't know," Jennie said. "But if not, we can always do it another time. It's not like this is the only time we could ever go over there."

"That's true," Patty said. She actually had a bad feeling about this, but was not sure why.   Patty didn't want to say anything, because she was afraid it might hurt Ami's feelings.

"Well, whatever they decide, we'll have a sleepover on Saturday. Where doesn't matter, so long as we're all together," Bobbi said, raising her glass of Pepsi.

"Hear! Hear!" The others said with a giggle.

Jan said, "I trust Ami. The only concern I have is in case of an emergency."

Elaine nodded. "I trust Jennie too. But what if some of the other kids find out and try to make some trouble. Ami is welcome to stay with us while you're out of town, Jan."

"I appreciate that, Elaine, and I might just take you up on that. I don't really want her to be home alone."

"Where do you live, Jan? I don't think you've said." Dennis commented.

"Every time I tell someone where it is, they tell me it's cursed. So, I'll just go and say that I live in the house that local superstition claims is cursed."

Elaine grinned. "No wonder they are all so keen to stay the night there. Spending the night in a cursed house. How exciting!"

"Hey, I live there every night. But seriously, nothing has happened. We redid the inside, and it's been really quiet."

Dennis shrugged. "It's only a mile from here. I could drive over a few times and check on them. See if they need anything."

"And I'll go shopping with Jan to make sure the house has the proper snacks for a sleepover," Elaine says. "I probably should check your pantry anyway, make sure you are stocked up properly."

Dennis slapped Jan on the back. "Welcome to the family. You're officially one of Elaine's strays."

Jan laughed. "I'm going to accept that as the blessing it is."

The three parents walked back into the dining room. Elaine Jennison spoke for the group. "Okay, we decided it would be okay for you to have a sleepover at Ami's house. Dennis will come by a few times to check and see if you're okay. And if you need anything at all, you call us immediately. Don't hesitate."

The girls cheered.

Chapter 6

The rest of the week was very busy. Ami found that Patty had worked with a local psychic after school to train her gift, but was no longer doing so. Bobbi and Lyn both made the basketball teams and she and Jennie had both made the cheer squad. They met at Jennie's after practice got out, worked for an hour on homework, and then helped Mrs. J finish dinner. Ami had learned how to make meatloaf this week.

After dinner, they finished any homework that they had not completed, did each other's hair, gossiped about boys, and had a great time. Near 8:30, Mr. J loaded them all in the car and drove them to their houses.

Ami stayed with the Jenison's on Friday night, as Jan had left town earlier that morning to head back to Santa Fe for a weekend meeting. He and Elaine had already gotten bags of groceries, which she helped them unload at the house. All of her friends would be eating really well tonight. He had also let her rent three movies: Dirty Dancing, Princess Bride, and Willow.

By 4:00, the five girls were at Ami's house. She gave them the grand tour, starting with the kitchen. She was extremely proud to show it off, and they were all duly impressed. Bobbi and Patty both loved the living room.

When she showed them her room, they were silent. "This is amazing," breathed Lyn. "I mean, it's perfect for you. I love all of it."

Patty, however, was staring at Ami's closet. "How did you get all of your clothes to match so perfectly?"

Ami shrugged. "I don't know. I didn't do it intentionally, it just kinda happened." She didn't mention that she had never noticed it before. It was one of the odd details from her dream, and that had been the thing that had been bothering her every time she'd looked in her closet. She just had not been able to figure out exactly what it was that had bothered her.

"I have something else I've been wanting to show you! Come on." Ami led them outside to the tree house.

"Wow." Jennie's statement summed it up.

"I thought we could hang out here tonight. We have a fridge, which is pretty well stocked, and we can always go in the house for more stuff if we need. There's a microwave, so we can have popcorn. And I rented some movies."

"This is perfect." Bobbi said.

"I can't believe this tree house. Did your dad build it," Lyn asked.

"No. It was here when we bought the place. We had to clean it up a bit, and Dad had someone come check and make sure it was safe."

Patty relaxed. "I really like this place. We should stay out here tonight."

"So, what should we watch first?" Jennie asked.

In the end, the girls decided that all of the movies had strong appeal, and put them in a bag to be pulled out at random. Ami popped two big bowls of popcorn and everyone settled into a spot. Then they drew a movie out of the bag.

The Princess Bride.

"I love this movie," Ami said.

"You've seen it?" Jennie asked. "I saw the trailers and really wanted to, but it didn't play anywhere near here."

"You are going to love it," Ami smiled. Now that she knew her friends had not seen it, she resolved to not talk too much during the movie. After the second time Inigo said "Hello, my name is Inigo Montoya. You killed my father. Prepare to die," they were all saying it with him. The girls laughed when Vizzini kept saying "inconceivable." And when Lyn had to go to the house to use the bathroom, accompanied by Bobbi, the others shouted, "Have fun storming the castle!"

Patty, Ami and Jennie sat in the tree house waiting for them to come back. "This is really fun," Jennie said. "I can't believe my parents agreed to this."

"Neither can I," said Patty.

Ami checked the small refrigerator. They had plenty of Pepsis. "I'm going to run to the house too, before we start the next movie."

"Probably should all do that," Jennie said. The three climbed down the stairs just as Lyn and Bobbi were coming back.

"Our turn," Patty whispered.

"Why don't you pick our next movie?" Ami said. "We'll be right back."

By the time they finished all three movies, Mr. J had stopped by twice. It was 10:30. They were having a great time. But then it started to thunder.

"I don't think we should be in a tree house in this weather," Lyn said.

Bobbi and Jennie agreed.

"I'm sorry guys. But you're right. There's plenty of room in my bedroom. And it's pretty cozy," Ami said

They packed up their sleeping rolls and quickly carried them down. Ami locked the tree house before they left. They got all settled into Ami's room.

"So, now what do we do?" Ami asked.

"It's your house," Jennie said. "What would you like to do?"

"We could tell scary stories, if you guys would like," Ami said.

"Ooh, that sounds like fun!" Lyn said.

Ami grinned. "Okay. Here are the rules, if you guys are interested. First, the story has to be about one of us. Second, the person who the story is about has to tell the next story. So, I'm going to tell a story about Bobbi. And then Bobbi will tell the next one. See?"

"So your story will be the last one, right?"

"Right!" Ami said. "It doesn't have to be about something that the person has done. It just has to feature one of us. But we should try to fit the scary adventure to the main character, if we can."

"Does the main character have to survive?" Patty asked.

Ami shrugged. "What do you think?"

"I don't think it should matter. After all, it's not like we want anything bad to really happen. It's just a story that we're telling," Jennie said. "So if it fits with the story, then the main character should die. And if it fits with the story that's being told, then the main character should triumph."

"How long should it be?" Lyn asked.

"As long as it needs to be," Ami said.

"I think we should vote on the best, scariest story at the end," Bobbi suggested.

"But what would be the prize?" Jennie asked.

Ami shrugged. "How about whoever wins starts the next time we do it. And she gets to have possession of this." Ami went to her stuffed animals and found a stuffed owl. "The owl must be brought to all sleepovers, and will be passed around."

They all examined the owl and decided it would be a good 'trophy.'

Everyone got settled. They turned out the house lights and turned on their flashlights. Lightning flashed across the night sky.

"Ooooo scary!" Bobbi said.

Ami settled in. "My story will be about Bobbi. Bobbi, I'm just using you as a character, so anything I say about 'you' is not really 'you' or what I think about you. Okay?"

"All right," Bobbi said.

Ami nodded and took a deep breath. She squeezed the owl she was holding. She was actually a little nervous about telling a story, but still she was among friends, and they were not competing for a literary prize. Just the right to start the next round-- and to hold on to the 'coveted' owl.

Chapter 7

Roberta Ann Jones, Bobbi to her friends, was a pretty girl. No, she was a beautiful girl. Easily the prettiest girl at Central High School. What's more, Bobbi knew it. To call her vain would be unfair. Because while Bobbi knew she was beautiful, she didn't feel like she had any other skills. She didn't think she was funny, though her friends would say she had a lovely sense of humor. She didn't think she was smart, though she did well enough on tests. She didn't feel popular--though everyone thought she was kind. Bobbi never acted like she was better than everyone else, just because she was beautiful. Bobbi considered it something that was just a part of her. Some people were wonderful singers. Some people were really smart. Bobbi was beautiful.

All she felt that she had was her appearance. So she made sure she took care of that. She never used soap on her face, as she didn't want to dry out her skin. She used face creams to keep her skin from drying out. And she almost never smiled, as that would give her wrinkles around her eyes.

To Bobbi, her only asset was her appearance--and she also knew that it was something that was fleeting. She wouldn't always be seventeen.

Her hair was a gorgeous brown, with just the right amount of body, cut in a modern bob. Her hair was all the same length and she kept it cut to just below her chin.

On days when Bobbi was feeling shy, she would wear her hair so that it covered half of her face. It was almost a mask for her. Bobbi loved the feeling of being able to see out, and being able to keep others from seeing all of her.

Still, because she was so very beautiful, Bobbi made enemies without even trying. Girls were jealous of her appearance. Bobbi knew this, but tried not to let it bother her. Maybe they thought she was aloof because she didn't smile often.

Bobbi had some great friends, friends who did see her as more than just the pretty face of Central High. These girls knew how kind-hearted and gentle Bobbi was. And thus, they earned enemies, too.

It started innocently enough. Bobbi received a note in her locker.

"too pretty girl"

Nothing else.

She couldn't tell if it was a threat, a comment, or a gift tag with bad grammar. Bobbi just put it to the side and didn't think of it again.

But a week later she got another note. It said the exact same thing. But this time it was written on black paper. Bobbi set it aside and went to class. Again, she forgot all about it.

When Bobbi got to class, she started to feel a pain in her right hand--a strong burning itch. She had an ugly rash on her right hand--the hand that had picked up the note. She didn't connect the two events. But someone in the class noticed and smiled.

The rash grew worse and worse as the day went on. It hurt badly. By the end of the day, it had caused the skin on her right hand to blister and bleed, to dry out and crack. Finally, she was in so much pain, she went to the doctor who was very baffled by the condition. The doctor prescribed a lotion anyway, to alleviate the pain if nothing else. He covered her hand with the lotion and placed a glove over the hand, telling her it had to stay on for twenty-four hours. She could take it off to apply more lotion, but the hand was to remain dry and covered during that time. Then she was to come back to him for further evaluation.

Bobbi stayed home from school the next day. She had no idea what she had gotten into to have caused such an awful rash. But she was extremely miserable.

And her absence from school was noticed, and someone smiled.

The next day, Bobbi went back to the doctor. He unwrapped her hand and smiled. "Looks like that took care of it. How does your hand feel?"

"Much better. Do you know what it was?"

"Clearly an allergic reaction to something." The two sat down and went through a list of everywhere Bobbi had been and everything she had done. They could find nothing at all unusual about what she had done recently. He advised her to keep trying to think of things that she had done, places she had been, things she had touched, that were out of place.

Bobbi promised she would.

When Bobbi returned to school, her friends were very concerned, but thrilled she was all right. They also tried to think of things that were unusual and came up with nothing. Bobbi had not mentioned the notes to them. Bobbi had forgotten all about them.

The next day in the cafeteria, Bobbi was sitting with a couple of her friends. They were eating lunch. Bobbi had brought her lunch from home as had both of her friends. Her dad always packed the same exact lunch for her. He had been packing this lunch for her ever since Bobbi could remember: peanut butter and jelly on rye, a bag of Lay's barbecue potato chips, a Hunt's chocolate fudge pudding cup, an apple, and a can of soda. He also always forgot the spoon. This was so common that one of Bobbi's friends always packed a second spoon for her. It had become a bit of a joke.

As they were eating, the friends were talking about what they wanted to do this weekend. Bobbi was interested in going to the mall in the next town. There was a new movie coming out that she wanted to see. Plus, she was also running low on her makeup and needed to get some new cover up. Her friends also both wanted to go to the mall, so they made plans for the road trip.

Bobbi started to put all of her trash back into her lunch bag when she noticed something. Inside of her lunch bag, at the very bottom, was written the words: too pretty girl.

She was so startled she dropped the bag. Her friends noticed her response and asked her what was going on.

She showed them the inside of her lunch sack.

"What's that supposed to mean?" One of her friends asked.

"I don't know. But I have gotten a couple of notes."

That's when Bobbi's eyes opened wide. "Oh. My. God," she said.

"What?"

"I got a note just before I got that really bad rash. What if something was on it?"

Her friends looked a little skeptical. "Wouldn't you have noticed if there was something on your hands? I mean, if there was a powder or some kind of oil or something, you'd have noticed and remembered that. But there wasn't, was there?"

"No."

"And did you only touch that note with your right hand?"

"I don't know. I don't remember. I just know this is the third time I have seen this phrase and I'm starting to get a little weirded out." She was very nervous. Someone had to have been in her locker to have written that there.

"Maybe you should tell the principal," one of her friends suggested.

"What good's that going to do?" Bobbi wanted to know. "Then they'll just be madder than before."

"But who are 'they,' Bobbi, and why are they mad at you?"

"I don't know!" Bobbi said, trying not to sob. She was scared, and actually starting to feel a little ill. Perhaps it was from the nerves. Or maybe because they had poisoned the food. Bobbi didn't know.

She stood up and the room started to tilt. Bobbi put her hand on the table, bracing herself against it. She felt hot and cold at the same time and was not sure how that could be. Her vision started to darken as she took deep breaths.

"Bobbi?" She heard someone calling her name, but it almost sounded as if it were coming from under water. "Bobbi? Are you okay?"

She was taking deep, gulping breaths. Fighting to stay standing, fighting to stay awake and on her feet, but she lost the battle as the room started to spin faster and faster, taking Bobbi with it to the floor. She was vaguely aware of one of her friends screaming her name as she fell, but she couldn't stop or respond.

And someone was watching. Amidst all the chaos in the lunchroom, with kids screaming, and teachers running in, then paramedics rushing in and taking Bobbi out, she sat there watching, a small smile growing on her face.

If anyone had noticed her, they would have wondered about her reaction. Bobbi Jones being wheeled out of the cafeteria on a gurney was certainly something exciting, something to talk about, but not necessarily something to smile about.

Bobbi's friends had been smart enough to take the lunch bag with them when they went with her to the hospital. They gave it to the doctor at the emergency room and told him what had been happening. He consulted with Bobbi's other doctor and Bobbi's parents. And Bobbi's parents consulted with the principal. They searched Bobbi's locker and found the two notes she had received before, and another one.

Clearly, someone was out to get Bobbi.

The paper on the second note was found to have some sort of acid on it, which caused the allergic reaction Bobbi had. And there were trace elements of poison in Bobbi's lunch bag.

An investigation developed at the school. Bobbi had a guard at the hospital, and only her family, and those few friends her family authorized, were allowed to see Bobbi.

She was pale. And she still looked unearthly beautiful. It took her a few weeks to recover from the poisoning. Her father was very reluctant to let her go back to school. Truthfully, Bobbi was reluctant as well. Someone was trying to hurt her and she had no idea who. But she was not someone who ran from her problems.

But the Bobbi who returned was a much different person. She jumped at shadows. She kept her head down. She didn't even smile in response to something someone told her. She barely talked to her friends, who tried their best to protect her. Bobbi was worried about when she would be attacked again, and if her enemy would ever have the courage to face her, or if she would continue to attack using the tools of cowards.

Bobbi now wore gloves. She carried her book bag with her, and kept everything with her at all times. She wouldn't use the lockers or touch anything. Bobbi was starting to become a recluse. Dark circles were forming under her eyes from lack of sleep, and there was nothing her friends could do to help her.

Finally, one of them said, "We were going to go to the mall. Why don't we do that this weekend?"

Bobbi hesitated.

"Come on, it's us. You know we love you and would never hurt you."

She reluctantly agreed and the three friends drove to the mall. Bobbi bought some foundation, and a new cream to cover the dark circles. They saw a movie and ate popcorn. By the time they were heading back towards home Bobbi had started to act a lot more like her old self. She was laughing more and relaxing more. Her friends were both very glad to see Bobbi relaxing like this.

They were worried because Bobbi's enemy was still unknown. However, she had been quiet for a while, and they were all hoping that the fact that the police had searched the school had made her realize what she was doing was wrong, and that she'd stop.

But they were wrong. While they were out of town, Bobbi's enemy had snuck into Bobbi's home. She had put something in Bobbi's shampoo. By itself, this was a completely harmless substance. It would go undetected. It wouldn't hurt Bobbi in any way. By itself. But she had another plan.

After she left Bobbi's house, she drove to the mall. She bought some foundation like Bobbi used. And she put something else onto it. Then she saw the girls going out to the car to put their shopping into the trunk. They were talking about seeing a movie. It was the perfect opportunity. She waited. She watched. The parking lot emptied out and the movie had definitely started. She worked the lock on the trunk and finally got it to open. Then she changed out the makeup Bobbi had bought with the one she had tampered with.

She grinned. Let Bobbi think herself beautiful. That would change. It would change soon. She had a plan that would make people notice her. She was pretty, very pretty. But no one ever said she was. No one ever noticed her. They always said how gorgeous Bobbi Jones was. And then they talked about how sweet and pleasant Bobbi was. Bobbi had made herself into a person that people wanted to hate, and then hated themselves for doing so. She was sweet and kind and nice. How can you hate that? She was just a jealous, spiteful girl, for disliking Bobbi for such a shallow reason.

But she didn't care. She hated her. And soon, they wouldn't say "Beautiful Bobbi." They'd say "poor Bobbi"...if Bobbi survived. And she dearly hoped Bobbi wouldn't.

The next morning, Bobbi took a shower and washed her hair with her tainted shampoo. But she didn't know it. She dried her hair and styled it. Then she washed her face and put on her makeup.

As the day went by, half of her face started to itch a little, and she wondered what was going on, but every time she looked at it, it looked fine. She had almost expected it to be red and blotchy.   But everything looked all right, so she figured it was just her imagination.

By lunch, her face had started to really hurt, but she could see nothing when she looked in the mirror. And it was only the part of her face which her hair had covered. Bobbi didn't say anything but her friends noticed that something was wrong. She was starting to withdraw again.

Bobbi had not seen anything that had a note on it but her enemy might have decided to keep silent this time and not give her any warnings.

Then one of her friends looked at her, her eyes widening. "Bobbi, how does your face feel?"

"It hurts....why do you ask?" Bobbi said. The last time she had looked, there was nothing wrong with her face. It was not red and there was no sign of a break out. It just hurt.

"Maybe you should go to a doctor."

"No, I don't want to bother them again," she said. "Besides, maybe when I wash my face, it will stop hurting."

"No, I don't think you should do that. You really need to go to the doctor, Bobbi. Now," her friend was insistent. And it looked like she was trying not to freak out. Her friend was staring at her and taking deep breaths. "Really."

Bobbi's other friend also had a very wide eyed expression. "I think she's right. Let's go now."

"What is it?"

"We'll just go to the hospital and have them take a look," she said.

"I want to take a look," Bobbi insisted.

"You really don't," they both replied. "Please trust us, you don't want to take a look." They tried to grab Bobbi's arm as she turned toward the bathroom. She was going to look into the mirror.

But they were both too late. Bobbi ran past them. She noticed the horrified looks of all of the students as she ran past them. What was so bad that she got those kinds of looks?

She ran into the bathroom, both of her friends running behind her, trying to catch her first.

And she looked in the mirror. Her hair covered half of her face, and she looked perfectly fine...except. There was something a little off. Just something not quite right. She pushed the hair out of her face.

And screamed.

The skin was eroding right before her eyes. She could see bits of muscle and bone as half of her face literally dissolved as she watched. She turned horror stricken eyes to her friends, who at least came and stood by her, even though they were clearly repulsed and terrified too.

There really was not anything a doctor could do.

But in the lunchroom, one of the students suddenly turned to another girl. "Sue Lynn, you look beautiful today."

And Sue Lynn smiled.

"Nice!" Lyn said.

"That ending is creepy," Jennie said, shivering. "I can't imagine being without half a face."

Ami smiled. "Thanks." She handed the owl to Bobbi.

"It's my turn, huh?"

Everyone nodded.

"Well, I doubt I will come up with something as creepy as having half a face dissolved off, and thanks for that image Ami."

"Any time," Ami said with a smirk.

Everyone laughed.

"Okay. My story is about Jennie. And part of it is based on our little Jennie here."

"Oooooo. This should be interesting," Patty said.

Bobbi grasped the owl. "I'm going to close my eyes. I don't think I can tell a story if you're all staring at me."

"Oh, no reason to be nervous. We're all friends here." Jennie said.

"All right. I just want to give you guys a good story."

"Just do your best. It's not like we prepared for this or anything." Lyn said.

Bobbi nodded, and she began to speak.

Chapter 8

Jennifer Michelle Jenison, Jennie to her friends, liked things fast. She drove her car faster than she should have...as fast as she could make it go. She liked to skate down the hill as fast as she could, feeling the wind in her hair. It almost made her feel like she was flying.

That was why she liked the speed.

It wasn't that she wanted to live dangerously. She just wanted to feel the freedom of flying, and the only time Jennie felt that freedom was when the wind was whipping through her hair, rushing past her face. It warmed her and made her feel alive.

Jennie drove a Buick Regal. Her father had taught her how to change its tires and oil, and keep it up. She had painted it a lemon yellow color, yellow being one of her favorite colors. She kept the car clean because it was something that was very important to her. How could it not be? This was her ticket to her rush.

When she drove to the mall at Mill's Valley Jennie drove fast. Every time she went her goal was to get there faster than the last time. She liked to beat her previous times.

Jennie's friends were always a little nervous while riding with her--but while she was fast, she was not a reckless driver. She never drove the car faster than she could control, but she drove fast...much faster than they liked.

But Jennie dreamed of a Porsche. She wanted to feel the power of a vehicle like that as she steered around turns. She wanted to drive the road of the Los Caracoles Pass in the Andes. The road was nothing but hair pin turns and switchbacks. To most people, it looked like a terrifying journey. But Jennie thought it would be fun. But, she wanted a car that was built to handle that kind of road.

And even though Jennie's parents were comfortably wealthy, they were not inclined to buy their daughter a car that was, as her father put it, 'death on wheels.' Truth be told, her parents were extremely over protective and had no idea that Jennie had such a need for speed.

Jennie figured if she was going to get the car of her dreams, she would have to get it herself. She took a job at the restaurant and put her love of speed to work. She was a great waitress. Her customers never complained about their wait. Orders went in quickly and were brought out as soon as they were done. Jennie made sure that her customers never had an empty glass and that their baskets of bread never ran out.

She put all of her earnings and tips in her savings account. She watched as the amount of money in that account grew weekly. But, she was also disappointed in how slowly it grew.

Her parents had no idea what she was saving her money for. If they had, she would have been forced to quit her job. The car was not something appropriate for her--and she had a perfectly good car.

Besides, how was she going to get to the Andes to drive up the Los Caracoles Pass?

Jennie figured she would worry about that after she had made the money for the car itself. She didn't say her dream was realistic, it was just her dream. And even if she couldn't drive the Andes, she could still drive her Porsche.

Jennie's parents wanted her to go to college and study to be a teacher. Jennie wanted to be a race car driver. Whenever she told people that, they laughed at her. Girls didn't race cars, they would say.

But Jennie dreamed of driving in the Indy 500, racing around the track at speeds unattainable by most cars. It was her most cherished dream. And she didn't care at all that girls were not supposed to do things like that. Fifty years ago, girls didn't go to college to become doctors and lawyers, but they were doing that now. Why shouldn't a girl be able to race a car? Why shouldn't she be able to compete with a man in this sport? It was all about how much power you could control.

And Jennie believed that having a Porsche would help her with that goal. It would take her one step closer. She planned to go to college in a town near a race track...Indianapolis would be ideal, but Talladega would be helpful too. In any event, she'd find someone who would teach her to drive that track. She was willing to work to earn her space on the track, but she wouldn't believe that she didn't have the right to try to live her dream just because she was a girl. That was ridiculous.

Everything was going along with Jennie's plan until one night when she left the diner.

There, parked next to her Buick, was a black car. It looked very much like the Porsche she'd dreamed of--but one she had never seen in any of the car magazines she read. It was shiny, new. But even as it shone, it also seemed to capture the light and almost keep it to itself. This car was something special and Jennie couldn't take her eyes off of it.

She walked all around the car admiring its beauty and style. It was indeed the car she had always dreamed of.

"Care to take her for a spin?"

Jennie jumped, so startled she let out a short squeak.

"I'm sorry. I didn't mean to frighten you."

Jennie turned around and watched as a man emerged from the shadows of the alley next to the diner. He was tall, very handsome, but she couldn't get a read on how old he was.

"Thank you, but I really shouldn't," Jennie said.

"Oh, but how you want to," he practically purred at her, knowing Jennie's truest desire.

"I do want to take her for a spin, as you say. But I shouldn't." Jennie tried to strengthen her resolve. I should not, she told herself again.

He held out the keys. "Take her. I'll wait here with your car."

Jennie held back, but the man didn't waver. He kept his arm extended, the keys dangling, held by his index finger and his thumb. He raised an eyebrow and watched her as she fought with herself. Finally, he smirked, as Jennie nodded and held out her hand. He dropped the keys in her palm.

"Thanks, Mister," Jennie said as she approached the car, feeling guilty for something she didn't really understand. Sure, she knew her dad would be extremely mad at her if he found out she had driven this stranger's car. But why would he need to know? If she took it for a short spin around the block she'd still be home almost at her normal time. And if she drove home quickly enough he might not even realize she had delayed leaving work.

Jennie got in the car. The leather seats were soft and creamy to the touch. The interior smelled of...cinnamon and musk. It was a heady and exotic aroma, and Jennie found it highly intriguing. She looked at the dash. Everything was organized so perfectly. She slipped the key into the ignition and started the car. The radio blazed to life with "Highway to Hell" and Jennie grinned. She listened to the engine as it roared. It was less like a kitten than like a lion. This car was ready to ride!

Jennie eased out of the parking lot and onto the street. She frowned as the scenery changed from what she was used to seeing when she drove. She was on a completely unknown road, and the car was bursting with energy, practically begging for speed.

Jennie gave in and pushed the gas pedal all the way to the floor. The car leapt into life. Jennie almost felt like she was riding a wild stallion and wrestling for control. The car almost had its own mind, but soon, the two of them--Jennie and the car--were of the same mind. She was one with this magnificently powerful machine and she saw a mountain looming in the distance. This mountain was not near her home. Jennie got a little nervous and turned the car around. Again, it was a struggle with the car, but she managed it.

Again, she hit the gas, and this time she thought of the diner in town. There it was just ahead. She pulled into the parking lot to find the man sitting on the hood of her car. Waiting.

Jennie was a little shaken by the experience. Shaken, but exhilarated.

She got out of the car and walked to the man, ready to hand him back his keys.

"What did you think of her?" he asked.

Jennie didn't know what to say. It had been weird.

"I have an offer for you, girl. An offer I don't think you'll refuse," he whispered. It was menacing and promising all at the same time.

"What...what's that?" Jennie asked.

"I'll give you my car, on one condition."

"You'll what? No, wait. That's not right. Why would you give me your car?"

He just smiled. "On one condition."

"Okay. What's the condition?" Jennie asked angrily. He was starting to scare her.

"Race me. You win, you keep the car. I win..." He walked up to her until he was standing right against her.

"What do you win if I lose?" she asked, stepping back.

"I win you." He took another step towards her. He was not touching her, not quite. But he was so close she could feel the heat of his body.

Trembling, Jennie stepped back again. "I beg your pardon?"

"You. You're my prize. You'll come back with me and never be seen here again." He pulled her to him in a forced embrace.

Jennie shook her head and struggled free. "No. You can keep your car." She threw the keys at him and ran to her own car, getting in quickly and starting the engine. He was still standing where she had left him.

He had an evil smirk on his face that told her she had not seen the last of him.

As Jennie drove home, she tried to decide whether she should tell her parents about that man. Obviously, she had made a huge mistake in accepting his first offer. But that didn't mean he should be able to treat her the way he had. She was not his, not just because she had driven his car. Of course, telling her dad would mean that she'd be grounded.

That might be a good thing right now. Maybe that strange man would leave town and she'd never see him again.

Jennie stopped in mid thought. She didn't have to be grounded to stay in. Sure, her friends might ask questions and her family might wonder. But there was nothing that would prevent her from staying home anyway. So she didn't have to tell her parents. Besides, the man hadn't done anything she could make a formal complaint about to anyone. Why should she get in trouble?

Having realized this, Jennie decided not to talk to her parents about the strange man. If any of her friends asked why she was staying home, except for school, she'd tell them. After all, she didn't want them to take that man's car for a spin. She needed to warn them about him because she didn't want him to be after her friends, too.

And it didn't take long for Jennie's friends to question her. She had quit her job. She wouldn't go to the mall with them. And they knew why she had the job in the first place, so quitting the job meant that Jennie was giving up on a dream, and they wanted to know what happened. So she told them.

Ami thought that Jennie should tell the police.

Patty grew very pale and wouldn't tell anyone what her concern was. However, she fully supported Jennie's plan, and felt that someone should stay with her all the time.

Lyn wanted to see the car.

And Bobbi missed the fun spiritedness of Jennie, and worried about her.

Of course, none of them had any solution for Jennie. So they stopped asking her if she'd go places with them, and just planned on staying with Jennie at her house.

For how long Jennie had no idea.

After two weeks Jennie figured she was safe. She hadn't seen the stranger, so she started to relax. She would go with her friends to the stores down town, though she did keep an eye out for the car.   She didn't see it. And she started to relax more.

Finally, Jennie felt safe again, confident that he had left.

One day, Jennie stayed late at school. She was working on decorating the gymnasium for a dance, and she was the last on the committee to leave. As she walked out to her car she was going over the plans for the dance later that evening.

By the time she saw him, it was too late.

"I told you, you will race me."

"I don't want to," Jennie said.

"Oh, yes you do. All you ever wanted to do was race, girl. Don't you think you're good enough?"

Jennie glared at him. "And my Buick is supposed to beat that car of yours?"

He shook his head. "Oh no. When I win, it will be in a fair race. You're racing to win this car, and your soul of course, so you'll drive this car."

"Who are you?" Jennie asked.

"You know who I am, Jennie. You know who I am."

"I think I do. But I want to hear you say it," she said, her voice full of false bravado.

"Oh, I have so many names," he said melodramatically. "Which shall I give you? Some call me Iblis, others Lucifer. The less creative simply call me the devil, Evil Incarnate."

Jennie nodded. "Why me?"

"Why not you?"

"Because I haven't done anything to hurt people. I'm not mean. I'm not particularly religious, that's true, but I'm not evil."

He laughed. "I don't need to win the evil, child. Those are already mine. People like you must be won. And the time for your contest is now. You can drive for your life or you can die now. The choice is yours."

Jennie frowned. "Fine, but I want to know the terms of this race."

Another car, identical to the one Jennie had driven before, appeared.

"You pick the car. They are the same, of course, and they will respond to the driver. I pick the course. And since I like the way you think, we'll race Los Caracoles Pass.   First one to the top wins."

Jennie raised her eyebrow. "In case you hadn't noticed, we're in Nebraska."

He smirked. "Sure of that, are you?"

Jennie looked around and saw they were not in Nebraska. They were at the foot of the mountain the car had approached the first time she drove it.

"All you have to do is beat me to the top. I win, you're mine. You win, the car is yours--and I'll leave you alone."

"I don't like this," she muttered.

"You don't have to like it. You just have to drive, Jennie."

The doors to both cars opened. Keys were already in the ignition. She just had to pick a car. Jennie walked over to one of the cars and got in. The devil did the same.

"GO!" he shouted.

Jennie felt her car roar to life. It wanted to win with her, at least that was what she hoped. She was trusting this machine with her life. She pushed the gas pedal to the floor and tightened her grip on the wheel as they approached the first switchback. It was tight, but Jennie surged ahead slightly. She kept up, pushing the car faster and faster. At the half-way point, she was a full switchback ahead of him, but she was not about to give up or hold back now. Too much was at stake.

Jennie started to believe that she could do this, that she had a chance of winning. But she knew the race was not over and the most dangerous part of any race was the other cars on the road. Just when she was starting to get into a groove driving this road, she saw some cars above, driving towards them. She managed the first set of cars, although several them honked their horns loudly.

Behind her she heard a crash. She forced herself not to look. She had to get to the top of this mountain, and there were other people whose lives were at stake here too. If she didn't pay attention to the road ahead she could hurt someone.

If she was going to die, she didn't like that at all, but she would rather be damned than kill someone else.

She could see it. She could see the top. And out of the corner of her eye, she could see another car approaching, a car that looked almost identical to hers. Jennie braced herself and held tight to the wheel. She gave the car as much gas as she could and held on tight. He might be upon her, but he had to pass her, and that she had control over. She swerved, covering the pavement, while watching the road ahead for oncoming traffic. It was clear for now, unless he threw anyone at her unexpectedly. But she could only prepare for what she could see.

Jennie drove to the top and parked her car at the lookout. She grinned as he stopped his car.

She rolled her window down. "I won," she declared.

"You did," he conceded. "The car is yours. And just to show you I'm a sport," he paused for effect. "I'll even send you home."

Jennie blinked. And she was sitting in the school parking lot, in her black Porsche. Her yellow Buick was gone, but she didn't care. She had raced the devil and won her soul...and gotten a car as a bonus.

She just wasn't sure how she was going to explain this to her friends.

"Wow. Great story, Bobbi!" Ami said.

"Yeah, I loved it. I thought for sure Jennie was gonna die."

"Me too," Bobbi said. "But I couldn't. I think the deciding factor was when she would rather lose than let other people die. I wanted that character to win."

"Me too," said Lyn. "These stories are so much fun. Ami, this was a great idea."

Jennie nodded. She asked softly. "How did you know that was what I wanted to do? I've never told anyone I wanted to be a racer."

"It just seemed to fit. You do speed a lot, Jennie, and since you're not usually reckless, it just seemed to me that there had to be a reason for it," Bobbi said.

Ami felt a little awkward. Jennie's story had suited her so well. But Bobbi was not really that vain. Of course, Bobbi had known Jennie for a lot longer-- all their lives. She had known them for a week.

Bobbi passed the owl to Jennie. "Your turn," she said.

"Whoo boy. Yeah, I realized that I would be next as soon as you started my story. I have been trying to think of something good." Jennie said. "This won't be as good as Bobbi's or Ami's, I'm sure of that."

"Jennie, just do your best. We're not grading you or anything," Ami said.

"Yes we are. We're deciding who gets to keep that owl. Does it have a name, Ami?" Lyn asked.

"I called him Hoot."

"All right. The story telling is to win the right to shelter Hoot for a while." Lyn said.

"True. But we're not going to flunk someone out of a class or something."

Patty said, "that's right. And I know groups of friends who have something that they pass along whenever one of them does something stupid. They have to carry that item until another person in the group 'earns' it."

Ami grinned. "We should get something like that...but something we pass along whenever one of us does something amazing or has something really difficult we have to do. Something that encourages us and shows us that we have our friends behind us."

"I like that," Bobbi said. "Next weekend, why don't we go to the mall and pick out something together. I don't think Ami should have to sacrifice all of her stuffed animals."

"And it doesn't have to be a stuffed animal," Jennie said. "Why not make it jewelry, like a ring or necklace or something. Something we can wear that we'll feel, you know?"

"Right. We'll find something perfect. Now you're just stalling, and it's your turn," Lyn said with a grin.

"Just for that, I'm going to do my story on you," Jennie said, sticking out her tongue.

Lyn grinned.

Chapter 9

Lynette Marie Andrews, Lyn to those she respected and liked, liked fire. She liked to watch the dance of the flames as they flickered red and yellow and orange, and occasionally blue. She liked the smell of it as it ate through wood. She liked the taste of smoke on the air. There was something about fire that entranced Lyn. It seemed magical and mysterious. It saved lives and brought death. Fire encompassed all.

She liked to save up the papers from her classes every year and have a huge bon fire at the end, putting papers on that fire, almost as a sacrifice to time itself.

Bon fires were a celebration to her. They were special.

And while most people viewed them as a time to take out the marshmallows and Hershey bars, Lyn watched them almost as if they were a sacred altar purifying the world, ridding it of mistakes past, and giving her a chance to start again.

Lyn never thought of fire as a dangerous entity. It was something to be respected--but not something she could ever fear.   It was what called to her spirit.

When she was in her room, painted in the vibrant shades of fire--red, orange, and yellow--Lyn always kept a candle burning. A candle burned all the night through, and she only extinguished the candle when she left for the day. It soothed her, almost as if the fire was purifying her, burning away her stress, her anger, her emotions. Making her stronger. She felt more calm and peaceful when she woke in the night and saw the gentle flicker of the candle's light. Artificial candles were not the same.

Lyn surrounded herself with fire. It was a fascination her friends didn't understand and her parents didn't like. Her brother found it creepy. Lyn didn't care. It was a part of who she was and it was important to her. Her friends accepted it and bought her new candles. They always bought scents thinking that maybe Lyn wanted to smell Burberry or

Butterscotch. The scents were nice--but the true allure was the flame.

One day, while watching the flame flicker on the candle, Lyn thought she saw a face. She had been working rather hard on a paper, and it was rather late. Lyn decided to call it a night. Obviously, hallucinating about faces in flames was a good sign that she was very tired.

That night, she dreamed about fire. This was not unusual for Lyn. Fire was frequently a part of her dreams. However, this time she saw people in the flames. People who danced to the music that the fire made as it burned. The crackling had notes and rhythm and the fire people were vibrant. She wanted to join them, but she just watched. Then one of the flames broke away from the circle and came towards her, beckoning.

Lyn nodded. She approached the fire circle, the dancing flames. Her host showed her the steps, taught her to dance the way that the fire did. Barely touching the ground, turning, jumping, moving so fast it was almost like a flicker. The ballet of the fire dance was intricate and beautiful. Lyn was startled as a blaring noise came out of nowhere. The fire scattered and Lyn awoke. She felt more alive than she had before.

As she got up, she felt warm despite the cool temperatures outside. Lyn wore a red tank top with a skirt. She noticed her hair had a reddish highlight to it, and decided she should definitely keep using the shampoo she had just switched to. It was making her hair glow.   And she really liked the affect.

As Lyn waited for the bus, she noticed that the other kids wore jackets, and were looking rather cold. But she felt quite comfortable in her summer attire.

"Are you okay, Lyn?" Jeremy asked.

"You just look a little warm and it's really cold out. Are you sure you're not sick or something?"

"I'm fine," Lyn insisted. But she got that response all day long. She had dressed for summer in late fall. By rights she should have been cold. She had worn a jacket only yesterday and complained about the chill on the air. Yet today, in summer clothing, she was mostly comfortable, if not actually a little warm.

She didn't feel sick though. She felt fine. She felt...powerful and light.

That night she dreamed of the fire again. The dance was a bigger one. There were more flames tonight. Some of them were blue and white, they were the brighter, hotter flames. Lyn looked down and saw she wore red. Her skirt was layered shades of red with just a hint orange at the fringe. Most of the dancers near her were red flames. Near their bodies they had a little bit of orange.

Lyn watched the dance and noticed that the flames had classifications. Reds were where she was. The next circle was orange flames. They moved more quickly and had a more exotic dance.   Yellow was dancing higher above the fire   They also had a different dance that was more intricate than even the orange flames were dancing. And as she looked up she could see the blue and white dancers. Barely. They moved so quickly that they were almost a blur to her. But every once in a while Lyn would see a face.

Still, she was dancing with fire. She realized that they had accepted her into the ranks of their Red dancers and she focused on the dance, on the fire they were building, reveling in the joy of the dance. She was amazed that she never seemed to tire. The more she danced the better she felt and the bigger the dance became.

Suddenly, an orange flame broke away and approached her. He showed her the steps of the dance of the oranges and then went back. He left her to struggle through them. There were several other red flames which were trying the new dance. They flickered between red and orange as they learned. Lyn was excited to try the dance, and saw her skirt was getting lighter, the orange trim expanding. It was still mostly red, but every time she successfully went through the new dance it would become more orange.

Then the alarm blared and she woke up.

That morning, Lyn dressed in orange. Her hair seemed to have more light and life. She didn't connect her dreams with the changes she was going through, but they were apparent to others. Lyn had a glow. Her friends were concerned because whenever she stood close to them, they felt warmer. And this was nice when they were outside, but standing next to Lyn was almost like standing next to a fireplace. There was a definite warmth coming from her.

But Lyn couldn't see the changes herself. She noticed things, like her hair looking much better. It had more body and more color, and was starting to look the way she had always wanted it to look; however, she didn't see why that was a bad thing at all. She was using a new shampoo and it was obviously working wonders.

But she had more color in her cheeks, a natural blush and glow.

As Lyn did her homework that night she watched the flickering of the candle flame. It really was like a dance. Except that this candle was alone in the dance and she started to feel badly for it. It danced by itself.

That night, she once again dreamed of dancing with the fire people. She was so enjoying this dream. It refreshed her spirit. But tonight when she danced, she noticed her dress was entirely orange. But her dress was no longer cloth, like it had been before. It was fire. The flames of her dress licked against her legs spurring her faster and faster. This dress was lighter and silkier than anything she had ever worn. It felt almost alive. Lyn now thought of fire as a living, breathing thing. It danced. It felt. It came together in groups to create works of art the likes of which most people could only imagine.

She looked around at her fellow dancers. She cheered as an orange was promoted to yellow, the next tier of dance. There were fewer blues and whites than the other colors, but it was still lovely to watch someone make his way up the dance, improving, learning, creating more intricately. Lyn was happy where she was, though she longed to learn the beautiful dance of the yellow flames. She was amazed they had invited her this far.

And as the night was nearing an end she was beckoned to try the dance of yellow. No one showed her the steps. Those she had to figure for herself. When she had them she would change, Lyn knew. She tried it once and flickered briefly to red, then back to orange. She tried again but didn't have them right. The orange movements were so well known to her they were almost instinct now. So she let her body do them as she watched the yellow dance.

But just as she thought she was ready to try again, the alarm blared.

This was becoming most frustrating. Lyn was not sure why it bothered her so much to be awakened from this dream. But she was clearly going through some sort of a spiritual quest in her dreams, and she always felt like she was just about ready to make a breakthrough whenever the alarm went off.

This morning was different. After she got dressed, Lyn danced. She practiced the motions of the Dance of the Yellow Flames until she was sure she knew it. It was important to her to know it.

She went to school. And she had changed even more. Lyn was blossoming into a great beauty. People were drawn to her like moths were drawn to flames. But she didn't let them stay close. She looked forward to the evening, when she would dream of the Fire People. They were more alive to her than her friends or her family. Lyn was changing. She had always loved the fire, but she felt almost as if the Fire People were calling her home. Had she been a spark that was trapped here, in life unwilling? Lyn didn't know.

Lyn slept. She went willingly to the fire immediately dancing the Dance of the Yellow Flames. Her dress burst into flames, yellow, as she did it the first time through. She exhilarated in the dance, she shouted with joy and exulted in the feeling of the yellow dance. It was such a beautiful, joyful dance that it filled her heart with happiness.

Round and round she danced, and she felt it change. The dance was easier, more exquisite, and faster, more fluid. She changed her steps, moved slightly differently, and her dress flashed to blue. Lyn smiled. She had not even watched the blue dance. She had just felt it. And as she looked around, she saw smiles on the faces of the yellow flames as she floated higher up. She was no longer dancing on the ground, but flying in the air, twirling in place.

Lyn looked at her arms. But they were not arms, they were flames. She had transformed as she danced, and was a flame herself. She was FIRE!

And how she burned. She danced, faster and faster, her blue colors darkened and lightened as she kept with the music which she could hear. She remembered hearing it when she danced with the reds, but the tune had been different. They were dancing together, but listening to different songs. It suddenly all made sense why they danced differently. But still, the overall dance was a masterwork. A masterwork for anyone who could see it.

Lyn pitied the mortals who couldn't see the beauty of the dance of the flames, or hear the music of the Fire.

She heard the alarm blaring and she thought about ignoring it, dancing onward, but she was not quite ready. Not yet. She didn't completely believe in the Fire.

When Lyn got ready that morning she put on blue. She had earned the color. She was fire; she felt more alive. She was not really surprised to see her hair was the vibrant orange of fire. In the sunlight, it glowed so brightly that if one looked hard enough, one would see the sparks of flame dancing a halo around Lyn's head.

Her friends looked at her in shock. Lyn glowed, yes. She was radiant, true. But there was a very frightening look to her eyes. If you looked deeply enough into them, you could see flames dancing behind her eyes.

And she was warm. It was cold out, but Lyn again wore summer weight clothing and she seemed almost uncomfortably warm. Standing next to her was comforting and disconcerting at the same time.

They asked her time and time again if she was sure she was all right, but Lyn was. She had never felt better. She felt as if she were in her element for the first time in her life.

That night, while she studied with her candles lit around her, she again saw a face in the flame. Lyn held out her hand and a spark leapt from the candle onto it. Lyn listened and she could hear the music this little spark carried. Lyn was not surprised by the spark's life. It seemed to brighten as she held it close to her.

When she went to bed that night she didn't extinguish her candles. The spark rested on her shoulder, comfortable against her skin. Lyn slept and she dreamed. She was a blue fire and her little spark was with her, orange to her blue. It danced with her in partnership until the music changed. Lyn danced a new song, changing her motions and feeling the transformation building up within her until it was about to burst.

She took a deep breath, increased the pace of her dance, danced with more frenzy than ever she had before, and felt it with a rush of satisfaction. She was white fire, flame of pure energy. Releasing her hold on the spark Lyn danced on. From her position as a White Flame, Lyn could see the pattern of the full dance. She could hear the entire symphony surrounding her. The separate pieces were each just a portion of the master symphony, but hearing it all together Lyn wept with joy. It was beautiful. It was the most beautiful sound she had ever heard.

Lyn didn't want this to ever end. She was one with The Flame. She saw that now. The Red Flames danced by themselves at the edges and the Orange Flames danced in partnership. Yellows danced in groups. But the Blue Flames danced within them all. The White Flames though brought the dance together, made it one choreography. It was this that made the fire build and burn. And Lyn was part of that now.

She didn't hear the alarm that morning.

Nor did she hear her mother's scream when she entered her room to find her bed on fire and Lyn gone.

Lyn was one with The Flame.

"Awesome! So Lyn spontaneously combusted or something like that?" Bobbi asked.

"Something like. I chose this because Lyn is such a pyro," Jennie said.

"Well, fire is beautiful," Lyn said.

Ami nodded.

"And I'm always careful with it," Lyn added.

"I know, that's why I didn't have the story where the main character got caught in a fire that went out of control," Jennie said, hugging Lyn. "Ami, in case you ever want to get Lyn something, get her a candle."

"Seriously?" Ami asked.

The others all nodded their heads.

"She really does watch the fire a lot," Bobbi said.

Patty said, "She once told me it looked like a dance and she was trying to figure out the routine."

"Wow," Ami said.

Jennie passed the owl to Lyn.

"Jennie, I liked my story a lot. Thanks! And now, it looks like my story will have to be about Patty, since Ami's tale is last," Lyn said. "So Patty, get ready because you're next."

"Yeah, I know. I figured out when Jennie started. I'm not quite sure what Ami's story is going to be about yet, but we'll see."

Lyn laughed. "I haven't figured out yours yet. We're just going to have to watch it grow."

They all laughed. Lyn was the kind of girl who tended to do her homework on the fly anyway. That was how she thrived, so making up a story should not pose any problems for her.

Chapter 10

Patricia Smith, known to her friends as Patty, was a little strange. Her friends didn't think of her as strange, but everyone else did. Patty didn't really blame them. She knew when things were going to happen, things she shouldn't know, couldn't know. But Patty did. When she was much younger, it was considered coincidence. But only so much can be called coincidence before people start to wonder, start to talk. And Patty was far past coincidences.

Truth be told, Patty herself could not deny the strange things she knew. It was almost as if she had her own personal television station telling and showing her things. She was already considered a freak because she was an orphan, and if Patty could turn off this knowledge she would. However, she had also accepted that she could not dismiss what she knew. If she was going to be a freak, then she was at least going to use that knowledge to help people.

Still, she was very happy that her friends did not consider her weird. They took her unusual skill in stride. Each of them was good at something, had a hidden skill, and they considered her psychic ability to be no odder than being able to run fast or sing. So, with them she could be herself.

However, she had also found that her abilities were getting stronger. She was getting more clear pictures more frequently than before.

Still, Patty was very surprised when she walked into the library to return a book. There was a woman sitting at one of the tables, quietly reading. But something about her was unnerving to Patty. She could not put her finger on it, so she kept staring at her. Still, Patty could not figure out why that woman was bothering her, what about her was not quite right.

It started happening more and more. Patty would see someone who looked out of place. They were everywhere. At the coffee-shop, in the park, walking down the street, even on the school campus. Patty suspected why they were bothering her, but she was not ready to test her theory.

Still, Patty had finally figured out what was wrong with these people. Their clothes were out of date. Not just last season's styles, seriously out of date. This town was around 100 years old, and some of the clothes looked like they were from that period.

Patty started to try to find out about some of the early settlers. She researched pictures at the Town Hall and even found some Carte de Visite and other old photographs. In there, she found a picture of the woman in the library. Josephine Carmichael. She had been the town's librarian and had never married. Her whole world, whole life, was that library. She had died in an accident at the library--one of the book shelves had fallen on her. Patty decided to see if she could talk to Ms. Carmichael, so she left the Town Hall and walked to the library. There sat Ms. Carmichael, in the same place as before, reading.

"Is it a good book?" Patty asked as she sat down next to her.

Josephine looked at her in shock. "You..."

Patty nodded. "Is it good?"

Josephine smiled. "Yes. I have read all the books in this library, but this one is one of my favorites."

Patty leaned over and saw that Josephine was reading "Wuthering Heights."

"I haven't read it."

"Oh, you should. I mean, it's sad, but really the story is so well crafted."

Patty nodded. "I'll wait until you've finished it, then check it out."

Josephine smiled.

"Are you happy here?" Patty asked.

Josephine shrugged. "There are worse places I could be. I am in a library. New books come in all the time and I get to read them.   Books I would never have been able to read. Books like Hitchhiker's Guide to the Galaxy."

"I haven't read it."

Josephine grinned. "You really need to spend more time in a library!"

Patty laughed. "You're probably right. Would you mind if I came and talked to you every once in a while, and got recommendations...what to read and what to avoid?"

Josephine smiled. "I'd like that. So, do you have any other spirit friends?"

"Not yet," Patty said. "But I'm working on it."

Josephine nodded. "Some of them are not very happy and would like to be somewhere else. Please be careful..."

Patty frowned. "Are there some I should avoid?"

"Unfortunately, if word gets around that you can talk to us, they will find you." Josephine looked up and frowned, watching the door. "And apparently, the word has gotten out."

Patty watched as a rather rough looking man strode towards them, paying no mind to anyone other than Patty and Josephine.

"You. Girl. You see us?" the man asked.

Patty nodded.

He relaxed. "Really?"

Patty nodded again. "Are you happy here?"

The man shook his head. Patty pulled out a chair and he filled it. "No. I'm not. You think you can do something about that, girl?"

Patty shrugged. "Mister, I don't know. I don't mind looking into it. What's your name?"

"Don't rightly know," he replied gruffly. "That important?"

"I don't know. I mean, it could be, but maybe not. Ms. Carmichael, would you be willing to help?"

Josephine looked at her. "So long as you understand that I am happy here and I don't want anything to change for me."

Patty smiled. "No, Ma'am. I'm looking for book recommendations. I promise, I'm not going to try to remove any spirit that isn't harming people, unless that spirit wants me to."

The man growled. "What about the ones that are harming people."

Patty leveled her eyes at him. "The way I look at it is this: if they are hurting people then I am going to do what I can to stop them. Got a problem with that?" she asked him haughtily. It was more bravado than an actual threat. But he grinned anyway.

"You got guts, girl. What's your name?"

Patty just looked at him and smiled. "I was not born yesterday. Names are power."

He just laughed. "So you and this librarian are going to see if you can help me out." Josephine relaxed.

"Yessir, I am, "she said to him, genuinely smiling.

"I know, I look rough. Mighta been rough a long time ago, too. But hangin' round gives a man time to think about who he was. Didn't like that feller too much, but I been changin'. Just can't change how I look now."

"That is probably why you do not know your name now. Who you were is not who you are now," Patty said.

He nodded.

Josephine looked at him quizzically. "How did you find out she could see us?"

"She's stared at me a few times. And at a few others too. Word is getting round." The man looked at Patty. "I'll do what I can to keep you safe for now. But you start sending folk on and there will be consequences. Best know how to send both those who are willin' and those who ain't before you try anything. Some folk ain't gonna take kindly to interfering."

Patty paled. "Right now, I'm not a threat. I'm just some weirdo who can see you. They don't know I can talk to you. And if all I'm doing is looking, they are not afraid of me."

"Xactly."

"Thank you," Patty said sincerely. The man nodded and turned and left. Patty looked at the librarian. "Guess I have a bit of research to do, don't I?"

Josephine nodded. "I don't want to go."

"Course not. For a bookworm like yourself, I imagine this is as close to heaven as you're going to get."

Josephine laughed. "I do believe you're right about that."

Over the next few weeks Patty researched and read books about banishing spirits--some were instructions on how to send those who were ready on their way and others told how to forcibly remove a spirit which did not want to go. That particular spell looked painful, and she resolved it would only be used on spirits which were harmful and causing disturbances. Spirits who were happy where they were and causing no harm did not need to leave.

After a few weeks Patty was finally ready. She knew both spells completely. She was ready to try it and see whether it worked. Patty looked around for the man. That was when she remembered he usually hung out near the auto parts store. Her research had told her that there used to be a bar in that location, so she figured that was where he had spent quite a bit of his life.

Sure enough, the man was leaning against the building when she approached him.

"Are you still ready?" Patty asked him.

"I sure am. Are you?"

"I believe so. I haven't tried it on anyone else though, so I only have my research to go by."

"Someone's got to go first." He fixed her with a hard stare. "You promise me you're just trying to help me move on, not banish me."

"I promise you that is my intent. I sincerely hope that is my result."

He nodded. "All right then If you end up banishing me, I forgive you."

Patty wished she could give him a hug, but all she could do was say, "thank you." "Mind if we do this some place a little less public, for me?"

The man agreed and they walked to the alley and behind the auto parts store.

"I need you to relax," she said.

He did and Patty started chanting. Soon, a vortex appeared. It was very faint for Patty but the man nodded. "I can smell daisies," he said. "And the name was Tom. Thank you, girl." Patty watched as he walked proudly through the gap and it closed behind him. She smiled.

And as she turned around she saw spirits coming up to her. Some angry, others hopeful.

Patty frowned then held up her hand. "I have no intention of sending anyone away unwilling...not unless they are harming people. So, if you're happy here I don't mean to send you away. Okay?"

Several spirits came forward, all shouting "Send me on!"

Patty was beginning to be overwhelmed, when Josephine came and stood beside her.

"You have waited, patiently or not, for a long time. This child cannot perform the spell limitless times in a single day. Each of you must have your own door way. So, she will help out and send three people home every week. It is up to us to determine the order."

Patty looked at her gratefully. She knew she could perform that spell several times a day, so she was not certain why Josephine limited it the way she had. Still, she nodded. "I will be here the day after tomorrow and will send someone home then. I will come here every other day until everyone who wishes to move on has had a chance to do so. After that, anyone who decides later will have to find me and I will help."

The spirits all nodded and left.

"Come with me. We need to talk," Josephine said, and Patty followed her to the library.

Once they were in Josephine's nook Patty asked her the question she had on her mind. "Why only three? I could do two or three a day."

Josephine nodded. "True. And if something happened where you needed to banish you'd have no energy. Plus, that much exposure to the spirit world could bring harm if not portioned out. This is for your safety."

Patty agreed. "Very sound logic. Thank you."

"Plus, they have waited. Knowing that they have the opportunity is enough. I could have said once a week and they would have been satisfied. Remember, we have a very different sense of time than you do."

Patty nodded.

Over the next few weeks all went well with releasing the spirits who wanted to move on. However, after sending off a little girl, a much more angry spirit approached her.

"Who do you think you are?!" he demanded. "How dare you!"

Patty was taken aback by his hostility. A few of the spirits had been turning up to send their fellows off, but when this entity appeared, most came and surrounded Patty. One even said to her: "He leaves the living alone, but he's been tormenting us. You're releasing his victims."

She was surprised.

"Is this why so many of you wish to depart?"

The spirit shrugged. "He is why I wish to."

"Stay behind me," Patty instructed. Then she turned to the angry spirit. "I give you a choice. Allow me to send you on your way willingly. Or I will banish you."

"You are a mere wisp of a girl. You cannot banish me. And I will not go."

Patty frowned. "I offered you a choice. This you have brought on yourself." With that, she raised her left hand and shouted an incantation. It was much harsher than the gentle one which she had been using, and a stronger vortex appeared. Patty could feel the wind whipping around her and the other spirits were touching her, grounding themselves. She directed her hand towards the spirit and felt her power bending to lift him off the ground, then she flung him into the vortex and ended the chant. It closed with a snap and the wind died immediately.

She felt drained and almost powerless. If another spirit like that came to her right now, she did not know if she would be able to banish him at that moment.

The others stood around her in awe.

"Are there others like him?" she asked them nervously.

They shook their head.

"Good," Patty whispered.

One of the spirits took her arm. She could feel some power feeding into her. "You looked like you could use a little. And you've given so much to us," she whispered.

"Thank you," Patty said. "If you don't mind, I might need an extra day before I come back."

They shrugged. "With him gone, I don't mind staying here," one said. Most nodded. "We'll find out how many more of us want to move on and let you know. Rest up for a bit, Spirit Warrior. We will wait."

Patty nodded as they faded. Until they were gone, she had not realized that they had Named her on their own. And it was truly a name of Power.

Patty was silent. The group was not sure if she was upset about Lyn's story or not.

"There must be something about this house," she said, reflectively. "All of these stories are so fitting, and about things we did not realize were important to each other."

Bobbi commented, "The house is supposed to be cursed. Maybe it's cursed to give the people in it a bit more intuition?"

Ami shrugged. "I don't know if I would call having good intuition a bad thing. I mean, isn't it a good thing when you can understand your friends...and what is bothering them?"

Jennie said, "It has been a bit odd. Some of these have been really on target about what we have said about each other."

"True, but mine was not true to Bobbi. Maybe you guys just really know each other really well, maybe better than you realized?" Ami suggested.

Lyn shrugged. "That's true. Maybe that's it."

"I hope so," Ami mumbled. She didn't like the idea of the house influencing them in any way.

Bobbi reached over and gave Ami a hug. "Don't worry. I'm sure the rumor of that curse on this house is just a bunch of local superstitious nonsense."

Lyn grinned. "Me, too. I might believe in a bit of psychic stuff but I don't believe in curses."

Jennie said something very similar. Only Patty remained silent.

Lyn handed the owl over to Patty. "Your turn."

Patty looked at Ami a moment, trying to come up with a good story for her. The last few moments had shown her that Ami was much more nervous about the possibility of a curse on the house than she wanted to let on. Patty had been thinking about doing a story on the house and Ami's fear.

So, she had to think a moment about whether she wanted to do that still. Ami had to live here after the story, and she was already afraid of the house. Jennie didn't live in her car. Bobbi's story was really good, but completely unrelated to her life. And how likely was it that Lyn would spontaneously combust and become a flame? None of these stories would really impact them perpetually. But Ami lived here and Patty didn't want to make Ami even more afraid of the house.

"I'm thinking," Patty said. "I had an idea, but I don't really want to go that way. Why don't we go get some more snacks and when we come back, I'll be ready."

"Good plan," Bobbi said. "We're out of popcorn."

Ami laughed.

Twenty minutes later, the girls reconvened in Ami's bedroom. They had popcorn, fresh drinks, cookies and leftover pizza. They got all settled in and Patty took up the owl.

"Is everyone ready," Patty asked, still stalling for time.

The other girls nodded.

"All right," Patty said.

Chapter 11

It was one of those days, Ami thought. Nothing too exciting was happening. So she decided to take a walk. She was new to the area, but Ami figured she would be all right as long as she didn't stray too far from home. She had admired the copse of trees behind her house, and she had not had a chance to explore them.

The weather was perfect for a walk, so Ami took a bottle of water and her Walkman, and headed outside. She smiled at the crisp smell on the air. This area was beautiful, with the leaves turning from green to gold and red. Ami saw there was a path and figured that it would be the best one to take. Ami figured it would be good to take because it would be easy to find her way back when she got tired.

Ami enjoyed the scenery, taking a leisurely walk through the small forest and enjoying the beauty. She watched as a few small squirrels darted across the branches of trees. There were a few birds flying through, singing.

Ami felt very peaceful and was really happy to find such a refuge so close to her home. A few steps away from her house was a bastion of peace. Ami wandered in farther and farther, not noticing that the light filtering through the trees had changed from a light green to a dark and murky dim. It was oppressive, but the change had been so subtle that Ami had not noticed until it was so oppressive that she felt trapped. The air was so thick it was hard to breathe and Ami was starting to feel very afraid. She turned around, planning to return along the path which she came by.

But it was gone. There were paths, but she couldn't tell which was the one she had come in by. Ami didn't know what to do. She knew she had not come very far in, but she didn't know where she was. She could try to find the right path.

But which one?

She looked at the paths and chose one. Ami hoped it was the right one and that she would soon be on her way home. She walked, looking around for signs of anything that looked familiar. Ami regretted that she had not been paying attention to specifics on her way in. She had been so busy enjoying the general scenery that she had not marked specific things--rocks which looked like faces, or trees that split down the middle.

But she didn't remember any creeks. And right now, there was a creek next to the path. Ami started to turn back, only to discover that the path behind her had disappeared. The one in front of her looked as if it were getting darker even than what she had been on before. She couldn't go backwards and she dared not go forwards.   Ami shivered.

She had not before believed in the supernatural. Ami, however, was starting to believe.

The wind howled causing Ami to shiver uncontrollably. It was not a natural sound on the wind. Should she leave the path or stay on it? Which offered her the best chance of getting home? Which offered her the best chance of safety? Right now, the forest was directing her steps, leading her where it willed, and she was feeling rather uncomfortable with that prospect. But she was also very uncertain about what dangers were offered off the path. Already she could hear things...but were they ahead of her? Ami didn't know.

Ami made a decision. If she was going to walk in to trouble, it would be on her own path. She stepped off the path and onto the forest floor. She walked about thirty paces before trying to evaluate which way she should go. Ami looked to see if she could still see the path she had been on, and she couldn't.

Now she was on her own and she was not sure how to proceed. But if she was going to run in to trouble it would be trouble she found all on her own.

Ami realized she had not heard the birds in a long time, probably since she had gotten away from the safer area of this forest. She listened hard, hoping to hear some in the distance to give her a direction to go.

The dark of the trees was oppressive, but she could still see a little. She just couldn't see far, certainly not to see any form of light in the distance. So she listened.

And again, she heard the howling, and this time she knew that it was not the wind which made such a fearsome noise. Ami was being hunted and standing still wouldn't save her. She had but one hope--find safety before whatever it was that was making that noise found her. She ran, hoping that it was in a direction that would lead her closer to home, but having no way to find that out. All she could do was run.

Ami watched the trees ahead and looked at the forest floor, hoping to avoid falling on the roots of the trees as they stretched out in front of her. Suddenly, a form darted in front of her.

"Follow me!" it called Ami was so startled she actually did.   As she ran, she watched the creature she was following. "Chessie?" Ami asked, surprised to see that she was following the cat from the bookstore.

"Yes, now follow me. We can talk in a moment."

Ami nodded. Talk? The cat actually was talking. This had to be a dream--a nightmare really--because cats didn't talk, or at least they didn't talk to her. Ami was not sure where her thoughts were going--she was obviously tired and letting her mind get the best of her. Still, she was not about to let Chessie out of her sight, talking cat or not. Chessie probably knew the way back to town and Ami was going to follow her as long as she could.

Chessie darted through the forest like a pro, jumping over things and giving Ami only the briefest of warnings when the ground was not level. But she kept a pace that Ami could match. Suddenly, Chessie darted down a hole.

Ami stopped and shook her head in shock. A hole?

Chessie came out and gave her a look of extreme frustration. "Are you going to follow me or not?"

Ami nodded her head while gaping a moment. She walked towards the hole, completely unsure how she would fit into a space that the cat was almost too big for. But she gamely went ahead with it, although she was not sure why. The howling behind her became louder, and Ami realized that while she had been focusing so much on keeping pace with Chessie, she had not been listening to the noises which had surely been gaining on them. She ran for the hole and jumped in.

And was amazed that she fit. Then she looked at Chessie. She was no taller than the cat.

"What just happened?" Ami asked herself.

"We'll talk later. Now keep moving," Chessie admonished. And Ami followed the cat through the tunnel underground. It was lit by some sort of a fungus or lichen. She heard the howling. It had stopped at the hole, but was clearly unable to pass through, and Ami breathed a sigh of relief.

Finally, Chessie stopped and allowed Ami a chance to take a break.

"Thanks," Ami mumbled.

She purred a moment. "Now, we can talk."

"Yeah, about that," Ami said. "I'm sorry, but I've never met a talking cat before."

"It's this place. I can't talk in town. This forest is dangerous and you should not have entered it," the cat said somberly.

Ami nodded. "I figured that one out. Of course, too late. As usual."

"I'm going to try to get you home, but it will be a little difficult. We have to come out of this tunnel where the magic still lingers, so that you can get the right size again. But there is a problem with that."

Ami looked at her. "Let me guess, it's in the area that's not exactly people friendly."

"You got it. So, I have to get you as close to the edge as possible, but not over." Chessie sat down. "You're very lucky I was out today."

"I'm very glad you were. It's not going to be a picnic through this tunnel, is it?" Ami asked.

Chessie shook her head. "But it's not too bad. Most stuff in here I can take care of. I can't beat that wolf, though."

Chessie indicated Ami should grab a root that was sticking out. "You might need this."

Now that they were not being pursued Chessie led them at a walk. She would pause every once in a while, to confirm they were going the right way, and Ami was a lot more happy walking beside her.

"How do you like being a book store cat?" Ami asked.

"It's good. Comfy chairs. Relatively quiet. People make their kids behave, and when they don't, I can jump on a bookshelf out of the way. Annabelle treats me really well, so I'm pretty happy there." Chessie winked at her. "But you can always bring me cat treats. I wouldn't mind those, of course."

Ami grinned. "Of course. Anything in particular?"

"I'm rather partial to tuna," Chessie said, licking her lips. Ami decided right then that she would always make time to visit Chessie at the bookstore, and she would always have tuna treats on her. Chessie had certainly earned that much by saving her this far.

Of course, if something happened here, there was no way anyone would ever find her--under the ground, the size of a Barbie doll.

Chessie licked her shoulder. "Are you ready?"

Ami nodded.

Chessie explained to her what would happen when they left the underground tunnel. "I'm going to bring you out, like I said, as close as I can to the edge of this part of the forest. When you come out, run straight. Keep running straight, no matter what you see."

"What if there is a tree?" Ami asked.

"Run straight. It's an illusion," Chessie said. "Don't veer even slightly, as the path back is very, very narrow. Run through trees. Close your eyes if you must. Don't follow me. Okay?"

"But why?" Ami asked.

"There will probably be something waiting for us. I want it to follow me."

"No, Chessie. I can't let you do that!"

She put her paw on Ami's shoulder. "Ami, I can come down here whenever I need. I will lead it away from you. You must run straight and not look back. I will be fine."

Ami nodded, blinking away tears. "All right. But how will I know how far to run."

Chessie purred. "You'll know. You'll feel it. If we're very lucky we'll come out close to your house, so you'll literally run out of the forest into your back yard. Otherwise, it will be close to town." She looked at Ami. "Don't stop running until you clear the trees. Don't run anything but straight, even when the trees look friendly. The forest will try anything to get you back."

Ami nodded.

"And above all, never come back into this forest again," Chessie admonished.

"I won't."

Chessie purred. "When I see you in the shop, I won't be able to speak. But I do understand you, so I don't mind if you want to talk to me, now and again."

Ami reached around Chessie's neck and gave her a hug. "Thank you."

They reached the hole. Ami could hear howling. Chessie set her on the path she was to go. "Now run. Don't look back. Don't turn. Run straight, no matter what you see. Believe nothing until you clear the trees."

"I will, Chessie," Ami said solemnly. She had gained a new respect for Chessie, in particular, and cats in general, from this. And she figured that if she got out of this experience, she wanted to ask her father if they could get a kitten. She might even ask Chessie for help in finding one. Chessie was smart; she'd find a way to show Ami.

"Good luck," Chessie whispered as Ami took off running.

Ami ran. A tree appeared in front of her and she closed her eyes and ran straight at it, full speed. In the distance, she heard the howling, and an occasional hiss. But, she didn't turn around or look over her shoulder. That would change her course-- and after all Chessie had done for her, the least Ami could do was follow the directions.

She ran until she was tired and her feet were sore, through rocks and trees, and into streams, but she didn't veer off the course and she didn't stop. Ami thought she could run no more, when she thought she saw the forest open to the left of her to a field. But Ami didn't turn. This was another trick of the forest, she knew it, trying to lure her to a false safety. Still, she kept running. The winds picked up, and the forest threw leaves and acorns at her, but Ami didn't stop.

Ami ran and ran, until her breath was ragged, and her shoes seemed to give out--and finally she ran out into a field of grass. Her house loomed in the distance. But she didn't stop running, not just yet. She ran and she saw her house getting closer and closer, and finally, she was home. She knew she was safe.

As she stepped on the porch, she looked back at the copse of trees. It looked so small and peaceful, but Ami knew otherwise. She smiled as she saw a small calico cat dart out of the forest and run towards the town.

Ami stopped momentarily, only to get a glass of water and change her shoes. Then she drove to the grocery store. She had some tuna treats to buy.

The next morning, Ami went to the book store, and looked for Chessie. Chessie was reclining in an overstuffed chair, where the sunbeams crossed. Ami sat down on the floor next to the chair. Chessie stretched and looked at her. Ami could almost see a smile in her face, when Chessie reached over and touched her nose to Ami's. "I brought you a thank you treat, Chessie," Ami said, and she took out a few kitty treats and gave them to the brave cat.

"I was thinking about getting a kitten. Any recommendations?"

Chessie looked long into Ami's eyes, then hopped down off the chair and led her to the cashier's station. There was a basket of kittens there. Chessie looked at the kittens for a moment before nuzzling one awake and lifting it out by the scruff of its neck. She carried the kitten over to Ami and sat it in her lap.

Annabelle looked over. "Looks like Chessie's decided to let you have one of her babies," she said.

Ami looked at Chessie. "I'm honored." She said as she petted the little calico kitten that had snuggled in her lap. "Truly honored." She smiled at Chessie. "Thank you."

Chessie nodded.

Patty put the owl in the middle.

Chapter 12

Ami grinned. "I liked that one. Mysterious and a talking cat. Plus a kitten. I really do want a kitten." She looked at everyone. "I guess it's time we decide who gets the owl."

"How do we do that?" Patty asked.

Ami shrugged. The popcorn bowl was empty. "Why don't we each take a slip of paper, write the name of the person who told the story we liked best, and we can put that in the popcorn bowl. Then I'll read them aloud."

The others agreed and Ami passed around sheets of paper and pens. Each person wrote a name down and put it in the popcorn bowl as it was passed around.

Ami looked around. "I just wanted to say that I liked all the stories."

Everyone else nodded. They agreed that everyone had told good stories.

Ami pulled the first paper out. "Bobbi."

Bobbi smiled.

The second paper also voted for Bobbi. The third one voted for Ami. The fourth was for Bobbi, and the last was for Jennie.

Ami handed the owl to Bobbi.

Bobbi blushed. "Thanks guys."

"I really liked that story a lot, Bobbi," Ami said. "It was spooky."

"All of them were. I hope I don't have nightmares," Lyn said.

"Me too!" said Ami.

They all nodded. The girls settled in to their sleeping bags. Bobbi hugged her owl. She was really very pleased by the validation of her friends. Bobbi wanted to be a writer, so for them to like hers best was thrilling to her.

They had big plans for the next day, going shopping and seeing a movie at the mall. They wanted to get up early, especially since their favorite store was having a huge sale. So they didn't keep each other awake talking. The girls were all soon asleep.

In Patty's dream, a woman she had never seen beckoned her. She was unsure about her; but at the same time, the woman felt familiar. She followed the unknown woman, keeping a bit of distance between them, just in case she needed to run. Finally, the woman went into the living room and took a seat on a chair. She nodded to the couch, indicating Patty should sit.

"Do you know who I am?" the woman asked.

Patty shook her head. "No. I don't."

She smiled. "I'm not surprised. I'm Ami's mother, Sofia."

Patty frowned. "I don't mean to be rude but--"

"Why am I here? Yes, that's a good question, and it's important for you to understand this." Sofia smiled. "I'm here because Jan, Ami's father, dreams of me every night, and is convinced he can feel my presence in this house. So...my presence is in this house."

Patty smiled. "Does Ami know?"

"No, not yet. She will need to know soon. But I'm telling you this because you girls have created a very bad situation for yourselves. And there was nothing I could do to stop it." Sofia looked at Patty gravely. "I'm talking to you, because I felt you would be the one who could handle this most quickly and with the least amount of panic."

Sofia frowned. "There is a curse on this house, as has been rumored. And I'm going to tell you what it is."

Patty was starting to get a very bad feeling, based on what Sofia had already said.

"This house has been cursed with truth. And while that does not sound like a bad thing, it can be. The house does not force you to speak the truth, or prevent you from lying. It simply takes what is said, what is thought, what is dreamed, and makes it come true."

Sofia waited a moment while Patty processed what she had just said.

"So...what you are telling me is that...oh my god!" Patty almost screamed. "Those stories. Lyn will die. And Bobbi..."

"Yes," Sofia said.

"No, that can't be right. I mean, they were just stories. And I'm dreaming right now. So this isn't really real. I'm just having a nightmare," Patty declared.

"Then this dream means nothing, and you'll wake up, and your friends will be fine. I wish nothing more than that were the case. However, I didn't come to scare you. So let's just assume for a moment that what I have told you is true. I came to you because I know how to help."

Patty nodded. "That sounds fair. If I'm dreaming, then it doesn't hurt to talk to you about this." She frowned. "I hope I'm just having a nightmare."

Sofia nodded. "I wish you were."

"So, what do we have to do?"

"This must be reversed before the sun rises, and I can think of only one way to do this. All of you must go to the tree house and you must talk there. Wake them up. Carry Lyn's sleeping bag over there and set it up, just as if she were in it. I will meet you over in the tree house, and we will talk about what must be done. Time is running out." Sofia paused. "Don't let Bobbi see her face. Wake Ami and Jennie up first and let them get over their shock."

Patty nodded. She ran up the stairs and looked in the room.   Lyn was missing. Ami held a kitten that looked up at her and meowed as she entered the room. After Sofia's warning, Patty was almost afraid to look at Bobbi. Bobbi slept on her side, her hair draped over her face, and Patty couldn't see it. She tapped Ami on the shoulder and woke her gently. Ami was a bit confused, and was even more startled when a kitten jumped up and licked her face. "Oh, hello little one. Where did you come from?"

Ami looked at Patty. "What's going on?"

"No time. Help me wake up Jennie."

Ami shrugged and woke up Jennie.

"Where's Lyn?" Jennie asked.

"No time," Patty said. "Wake up Bobbi, and don't stare at her. Don't let her look in a mirror and try not to let her touch her face."

"Patty, what is going on?" Jennie demanded.

"I'll tell you. But not here and not right now. Get your sleeping bag rolled up. We have to go to the tree house. I'll explain everything there."

The two girls shrugged and started packing up their bag. Jennie woke Bobbi up. When Bobbi sat up, her hair moved away from her face, and Jennie took a sharp intake of breath. Patty shook her head. "Bobbi, we have to get back to the tree house. I'll explain when we get there. Please pack up your sleeping bag."

"Where's Lyn?" Bobbi asked.

"No time. I promise, I'll explain everything." Patty had packed up her own sleeping bag and was working on Lyn's. "We have to go. Now."

She rushed them across the yard and into the tree house. It was a couple hours until the sun would be up, and Patty knew that they were running out of time. Patty had them lay their sleeping bags out like they had been in Ami's room.

"Ami, I'm sorry. There is a curse on your house. And you're about to get a shock."

"What? Another one?" Ami was still holding onto the kitten and doing her best not to look at Bobbi. Bobbi, for her part, was trying to figure out why her face hurt.

"Don't scratch that," Jennie said as Bobbi reached for her face.

"It hurts."

"Well, that's because you got bit by something last night," Jennie lied smoothly, causing Ami's eyes to widen. "You'll have to have a doctor look at it tomorrow, but until then, please leave it."

"Got a mirror up here, Ami?" Bobbi asked.

"No," Ami lied.

Bobbi shrugged. The three friends were trying to keep from her that she was missing half of her face and looked horrific.

Patty looked at them. "You wanted to know what was going on. Jennie, did you happen to notice the black car in the driveway?"

Jennie nodded. "And of course, Ami has noticed her kitten," Patty continued. "And that Lyn is missing."

"We don't have much time, so I'm sorry about this. Sofia, we need you now."

Ami looked at Patty like she had lost her mind, but only for a moment. Because in that instant, her mother, Sofia, appeared in the tree house.

"Everyone, this is Ami's mom, Sofia."

They all muttered nervous hellos as they looked at Patty. "What's going on?" Bobbi finally asked.

"The house is cursed with truth. Sofia's here because your dad dreams of her all the time and believes she is a presence in the house. So, she is." Patty took a deep breath. "The black car is Jennie's, from the story Bobbi told. As the kitten is Chessie's. Lyn is missing because she's where ever Jennie's story took her."

Bobbi gasped. "And my face hurts because it's half missing, right?"

Patty nodded. "I'm sorry."

"Can we fix this?" Ami asked.

Sofia nodded. "Yes, but we only have until the sun rises."

"What do we have to do?" Jennie asked.

"And can we remove the curse from this house?" Bobbi asked.

"We can remove the curse later. First we have to save Lyn and heal Bobbi," Patty said.

"I'm so sorry, Bobbi," Ami said. "I really am."

"Look, we'll talk about that later. I know you didn't do it on purpose, so let's just see what we can do, okay?" Bobbi said.

Ami nodded, still feeling horribly guilty, as did Jennie.

"What do we have to do?" Jennie asked again.

Sofia looked at them. "You must come up with a scenario, a believable one, that Ami can think. It would be best if we hypnotized her with it, so there is no chance of her straying from it. Ami, are you okay with that?"

"Mom, I have to do whatever I can to make this right. These are my friends!"

"That's my girl. Okay, we don't want to deviate too much--or the house might just ignore everything. It must be simple."

Bobbi looked at them. "I have an idea. Let me know what you think. We make Ami believe that instead of going into the house last night, we stayed here. So we still told those stories, and we'll all remember them. However, in the middle of the night,

Ami had to get up. She went to the house, but because she was only half-awake, she went back to bed like she always would. And she had a nightmare that this was real. When she woke up, she realized it was just her imagination running away from her and a dream, and all of her friends were safe in the tree house."

They all looked at Sofia. "Will that work?"

"I don't know," Sofia said. "The house makes dreams come true, so even if Ami believes that she had this nightmare, it might not be enough to have her realize it was a dream and everyone is safe."

They all thought. The clock was ticking and time was running out. They didn't have the luxury of time to decide what to do.

"Bobbi, this affects you and Lyn the most," Ami said softly. "And Lyn's not here. So what do you think? Should we go with your idea?"

"There's no guarantee it will work," Patty said.

"There's no guarantee any of this will. But we've got to do something. Time is running out, and I'd rather try something," Bobbi said, stoically.

Ami nodded and looked at Patty and Sofia. "How do we do this?" It was her only hope of saving their lives.

"If it works, we won't have anything but Ami telling us her nightmare. I think we need something to compel Ami not to talk about it in the house," Jennie said. "We probably need something to make us all unwilling to talk in her house. And Ami needs to not stay there until we can reverse the curse."

"Absolutely!" Bobbi said. "We can't let that house harm anyone else. That's a given."

Patty always wore a crystal necklace. It was a piece of rose quartz, cut as an obelisk. She wore it on a gold chain. Patty pulled the necklace out and looked at Ami.

"I want you to relax. Focus on this crystal. Everyone else, keep quiet. Ami, focus on the crystal and my voice. Only focus on these two things. I want you to relax and take deep breaths. Are you relaxed?"

Ami nodded.

"I want you to think of a beach. The sun is shining; it's warm, but not uncomfortable. The waves are lapping softly against the shore. Can you hear them?"

Ami nodded.

"Do you see the beach?"

Ami nodded.

"On that beach is a chair. It's sitting underneath an umbrella. I want you to walk towards the chair. Tell me when you have arrived at the chair."

Ami paused a moment, then said "I'm here."

"Okay, I'm going to count backwards from ten, and when I get to one, you're going to be sitting in that chair. Are you ready?"

Ami nodded.

"Ten, nine, eight, seven, six, five, four, three, two, one. Are you sitting?"

Ami nodded. As Patty had counted down, she and Jennie had helped Ami out of the tree house.

"I'm going to tell you a story. This story is the truth. It's the absolute truth. You believe this is the truth. Do you believe me?" They were walking her towards the house.

"Yes."

"Your friends are sleeping in your tree house and you are in your bed. You are in your bed because you went inside in the middle of the night and forgot you were outside. You had a nightmare that the stories told last night became true. But, it was only a nightmare. Your friends are safe in the tree house, all of them, they are sleeping. Do you believe this?"

"Yes."

"Where are your friends?"

"They are all safe and sleeping in the tree house," Ami said.

Patty looked at Jennie and sent her back to the tree house. She took Ami's arm. They stood in front of the house. "You will remember that this was a nightmare as soon as you wake up, and you will say the following statement out loud: It was only a nightmare. My friends are all safe in the tree house."

Ami nodded.

"Repeat the statement."

"It was only a nightmare. My friends are all safe in the tree house."

Patty walked Ami inside but said nothing more. She tucked her into bed. "You are beginning to wake up. When I tell you, you will count to twenty, and wake up fully. When you wake up, you will immediately say the phrase I told you. Nod your head if you understand."

Ami nodded her head.

"All right. Count to twenty."

Ami started to count to twenty, as Patty ran out of the room and through the house. She had to get up to the tree house before Ami was fully awake.

If Ami was successful she would probably not remember any of this.

Ami counted. One, two, three, four, five, six, seven, eight, nine, ten, eleven, twelve, thirteen, fourteen, fifteen, sixteen, seventeen, eighteen, nineteen, twenty. She woke up. "It was only a nightmare. My friends are all safe in the tree house." She frowned. That was an awful dream and she was glad it was only a dream.

"Why am I here?" Ami wondered, then she remembered that she had had to use the rest room in the middle of the night, and must have returned to the bedroom without thinking about it.

She walked downstairs and went out to the tree house to wake up her friends.

They were all asleep in the tree house. Safe.

Ami sat down on her sleeping bag, and Patty woke up and looked at her. "You are not going to believe the nightmare I had," Ami said.

Patty yawned. "Tell me about it," she said.

When Patty spoke, Jennie woke up and looked at Ami. "You are up way too early. Sun's not even up yet."

Ami nodded.

Bobbi pulled the sleeping bag down. "Why are we talking now?" she said with a yawn.

"I don't know, but someone better have some chocolate to make up for it," Lyn said.

"I had the weirdest dream," Ami said, "Nightmare really. It was really awful."

"Well, since we're awake, you might as well tell us what happened," Bobbi said.

"Remember the stories we told last night?" Ami asked.

"How could I forget," Lyn said. "Gave me nightmares. I felt like I was lost in a forest all night being chased by something howling. Thanks Patty."

"That was better than my nightmare," Ami said. "I dreamed that all of the stories came true, and that you were dead, and Bobbi was horribly disfigured. Sorry about that, Bobbi. And Jennie got a car, and I got a kitten."

"Wow," Jennie said. "That would be horrible! Not the car and the kitten, but Lyn being...oh wow. And Bobbi having her face half gone." She shuddered.

Patty was silent. She was looking over Ami's shoulder. Sofia was standing in the doorway, nodding. It had happened, and they had somehow fixed it. Patty could almost remember what had happened. Ami might think of it as a nightmare but

Patty knew it was not. It had happened and they had been able to reverse it.

Patty, Jennie, Ami and Bobbi looked at one another. It had happened. It was not a nightmare. They had just managed to reverse the dream, this time.

"Um, Ami, I really think your house is dangerous. You shouldn't stay there, not until we figure this out," Patty said.

"I agree," Jennie said. "You can't stay there. There is a curse on your house and we have got to figure out how to undo it."

Ami nodded. "I'm actually afraid to go in there. I just feel like we have gotten lucky, and until I can shake off how real it felt, going in there might make it happen again. I can't risk that with you."

Sofia stepped into their midst. "You're right."

That Ami didn't act surprised, only furthered their belief.

Lyn asked, "Um. Guys. Who is that? And is she what I think she is?" Her voice was very shaky.

Ami looked at Lyn. "Lyn, this is my mother Sofia. And yes, she's a ghost."

Lyn nodded and had a wry expression on her face. She spoke softly. "Okay. Just checking." She looked at the rest of her friends. "Any particular reason why I'm the only one freaking out?"

Bobbi looked at Lyn. "Because we met her last night, at least I think we did. Lyn, you don't remember because..."

"Because until this morning I was dead, too. Great. This is not how I wanted to start a Sunday."

Patty couldn't help it. She giggled. "Better confused than dead."

They all started laughing and soon even Lyn was laughing with them. It was the only way they could relieve the tension they all felt.

Jennie looked at Ami. "You have a good point. I don't think it's safe to go in there for a while. At least, not until we have a lot of other things on our minds to keep us distracted. We'll pack up here and head to my place. Ami, you can borrow some of my clothes."

"Thanks."

Sofia stopped them. "What were you planning on doing today? Before, I mean."

Bobbi shrugged. "We had planned on going to the mall, catching a movie, and eating at the Taco Bell."

"Do that. Get your life back to feeling normal as quickly as possible. I will be in the house, trying to figure out how the curse can be lifted."

Ami frowned. "Um, mom, isn't that dangerous? I mean, what if you think something or say something and it comes true."

"I'm a ghost. Those rules don't apply to me."

"Are you sure?" Patty asked.

Sofia nodded. "I figured out the curse a while ago, but I needed a bridge to get Ami to see me. And many a time I would say 'Ami can see me.' Then Ami would walk right past me as if I were not there."

"But now, will I be able to see you?" Ami asked.

"I don't know, dear. It might be you can only see me if Patty is here. She does have a strong psychic signature, so that might be why you can all see me. In any event, I will be around as long as I can." She grinned at the girls. "I want you to have fun today. Enjoy being alive. Take that from someone who knows."

They all nodded. Within a few minutes the tree house was cleaned. Their sleeping bags were stored in the corner. They each grabbed a Diet Coke from the refrigerator and headed down the steps.

They had walked about halfway to Jennie's when Jennie's dad pulled up to them. "Going somewhere?"

"We were just on the way home, Dad. Care to give us a lift?" Jennie said.

They had all agreed that their parents didn't need to know about last night's adventure.

Chapter 13

The girls rode in Jennie's car to the Mill's Valley Mall. They had been planning on watching "Nightmare on Elm Street" today, but there was no way any of them would watch that one for a while. They'd already had their own nightmare, and it was best if they kept Freddy far away. Right now, scary movies were off of the 'watch list' until they had this curse handled.

"I heard 'Young Guns' was coming out soon," Bobbi said. As an Emilio Estevez fan she had been wanting to see this movie. The others had not been quite as enthusiastic; however, it would keep their mind off of last night, and there were several really cute guys in the movie.

"If it's playing, I'm good with that one," Ami said.

"Yeah, me too," said Lyn.

"Done then," Jennie said with a giggle. "There's the majority already. What do you think Patty?"

"Seems like a good one to see." She spoke softly. "We also need to go to a book store. We might be able to find some things to help us with that curse."

"All right," Lyn said. "That sounds like a good plan. Should we do that instead of the movie?"

Ami shook her head. "No. We have got to do something to get our head out of that, too. If we don't try to go about normal, we're not going to be able to go inside. Our minds have to have something else to focus on, at least for a while."

Patty nodded. "Right. And what better way to get back to some kind of normal than to watch some hunks in cowboy hats, right?"

"Right!" they all shouted.

By the time they arrived at the mall, they were all a little hungry. It was still too early for lunch, and the movie wouldn't start for another hour. The girls decided to head to the food court to see what they had available. There was an Orange Julius, a Boardwalk Fries, and a Cindy's Cinnamon.

"Oooo cinnamon rolls!" Ami said excitedly. "I haven't had one of those in a while. Anyone want to share?"

"I'll split with you," Patty said.

Soon it was decided that Jennie and Lyn would split another. Bobbi wanted an Orange Julius.

They were a little skittish still, so they waited while Bobbi got her Orange Julius, then Bobbi followed the others over to Cindy's Cinnamon. They all got coffee, and then Patty and Ami got a cinnamon roll, and Jennie and Lyn got another. The five girls found a table and sat down to enjoy their treats.

As they ate they looked around the mall.

"I just got here, you know. When is homecoming, and will we have a dance?"

"Oh yes, there will definitely be a dance," Jennie said. "Have you met any of the guys yet?"

"A couple. Some seemed nice, but no one I'm really interested in yet. Is there anyone I should avoid?" Ami asked.

Patty shrugged. "There are a couple of guys that one of us has dated in the past. And those are usually off limits, but not because of jealousy or anything."

Ami looked at her.

"Well, for example, if I knew that Jack treated Jennie like crap, why would I want to date him?" Patty asked.

"That's a good point," Ami said.

"Of course," Lyn said, "Guys are guys, and they sometimes mature. Mind you, I said sometimes. Doesn't happen often, of course," she giggled.

"Anyway, there's only like three guys we would really want to steer you away from. They're mega jerks, and one has a reputation for bullying his girlfriends," Bobbi said.

"Don't need that kind of drama in my life, that's for sure!" Ami agreed.

"Now, tell us who you think is cute!" Jennie said.

Ami shrugged. "Kyle seems like he's nice."

"He is, but he's got a girlfriend over in Mesa City." Lyn said

"Good to know," Ami commented. "And George was kind of flirting with me," Ami added.

"And he's one of the mega jerks." Lyn stated.

"What about Chris?"

"Chris? Well, he's nice. But he's not the type to have a girlfriend. So, if you want a date for the dance, he's a good choice, but if you're looking for a boyfriend, keep on looking," Jennie said.

Ami nodded. "Right now, I have enough to worry about without a boyfriend on top of everything else. Should we go shop for dresses for homecoming?"

They finished their snacks. "I'd like to," Jennie said. "I just don't know..."

Patty smiled. "I usually don't go to dances, and she doesn't want to waste my time while you look for something to wear."

"Why not?" Ami said. "If you don't mind answering."

"Because no guy will ask me," Patty said.

"The psychic thing?" Ami asked.

Patty nodded. Ami reached over and gave her a hug. "Then they are just stupid jerks who are dumb. I know that's redundant, and I don't care. You're sweet and they'd be lucky to go to the dance with you. Besides. Is it required to have a date, or can't we go alone?"

Patty looked at her in shock. "No one does."

"So?" Ami said.

Jennie and Lyn nodded. "Yeah. Why shouldn't we? We can all go together. If a guy asks, fine. But if not, big deal."

Ami smiled.

The girls looked around at a few dresses, but didn't find anything they really liked. Then it was time for the movie. They bought their tickets, and each got a bag of popcorn and a drink. Ami got Whoppers. Patty got Milk Duds. Lyn and Bobbi each got Twizzlers. And Jennie got Snow Caps. They found their seats and waited for the movie to begin.

   It was a really fun movie, and had truly helped them to take their minds off of Ami's house. By the time they left, they were ready to hit the book store.

   "What are we looking for, Patty," Jennie asked.

   "I don't really know. Look, I know this may sound arrogant, but I'm pretty sure that I'll know it when I see it. Why don't you guys just look around at whatever you like to read? I'll try not to take too long, but I can't imagine it would take more than an hour--if they have it," Patty said.

   "Just call out if you need help. I don't want to be in your way," Ami said.

   "I don't mean it like that," Patty said.

   Ami smiled. "We know you don't. But you'll find it more quickly if we're not showing you things that are pointless, and we don't know what we're looking for. It's hard to describe what you have not seen, right?"

"Right. Thanks for understanding." Patty said.

"No. Thanks for trying to fix my house!" Ami said.

"I can't imagine any of us being willing to let that go, not if we can help!" Patty said.

"I know," Ami replied. "Good hunting," she said as she headed to the fantasy section of the book store. Bobbi and Lyn were already in romance and Jennie was shopping in self-help.

Meanwhile, in the occult section, Patty had decided to try unconventional means to find her book. She closed her eyes and concentrated on what she needed. Then she started to run her fingers slowly over the book spines. She was trying to find the book that would have something to help her with Ami's house. Anytime she got a slight tingle, she pulled the book and set it to the side. But she kept going. She would look at the books themselves after she had finished going through the shelves.

After her first run through, she had seven books.

Patty looked at the books that she had picked out. None of them could be ruled out immediately, and she might have to ask the others if they would help her buy them all.

However, before she did that, she wanted to have another 'look' at them. Patty closed her eyes and opened the first book. She skimmed over the table of contents and opened random pages to see how it felt. This book gave off a strong feeling. She set it to her right side.

She did the same with the next book. It gave off a strong feeling during one chapter, but other than that, nothing. Patty stopped and read that chapter. She wanted to see if there was perhaps anything worthwhile in that book. The book did talk about removing curses. Most of it talked about how the person who was the target of the curse needed to be the primary initiator of the removal.

However, in this case, there was not a person who was target. It was an object which was cursed. Because of this, the person or people in possession first needed to undergo some psychic cleansing.

That meant that they would need to involve Ami's father, Jan, in whatever they decided to do. However, the book itself had little else to offer, so Patty put it to her left side, as a book that she wouldn't be purchasing.

When Patty picked up the next book, it practically vibrated. She could tell that this was going to definitely need to come with her. She put it to the right immediately.

By the time Patty had finished sorting, she had three books in the 'buy' stack, and four that she needed to return to the shelf. This was actually a really good find. Patty returned the books they wouldn't be buying, and went over to the stationary portion of the store. There, she picked up a simple notebook. This would be used just for working on Ami's house.

"Find anything?" Ami asked as she walked up to Patty.

"A few things." Patty showed Ami the stack of books in her arms. "And we're going to have to go to an herbalist to get some supplies."

"Wow." Ami frowned. "Let me go get those." She reached for the books.

"No," Jennie said. "I think we should all pay for them. Patty, you're going to be paying with your energies, if I'm not mistaken, so the rest of us will pick up the tab for the books and any supplies you deem necessary."

"I--"

Bobbi looked at her. "Patty, you're not getting these frivolously. And whatever the price, it's worth it. We've got to make that house safe again--for all of us. I can't remove the curse. I know you can. I believe in you."

"So do I," said Lyn.

"Me too," added Ami.

"And me," finished Jennie. "We all believe in you. And I'll say that in that cursed house too, just to give us more strength in our beliefs!"

"That's right. We can use the house against itself, until we're ready," Bobbi said. "Not for personal gain or anything, but definitely to give us an advantage."

Patty frowned. "I'm afraid if we do that, it might negate the work we have to do. Trust me, when we start, that house is going to fight back. If we're very lucky, the person who cursed it won't know and show up."

Ami gasped. "They could do that?"

Patty shrugged. "Sometimes, when there is a personal aspect of a curse, the caster can feel when a curse is tampered with or lifted. Of course, if we're very lucky, she won't be able to do anything about it until it has been protected."

"I didn't realize it would be so dangerous," Ami whispered, horrified.

"It is. But I'm willing to take the risk," Patty said without hesitation. "I really am."

Ami nodded. "I wish we had never bought that house," she said, her voice full of unshed tears.

Jennie reached over and hugged her. "I know. But I'm not sorry you moved here. And besides, if you hadn't bought it, someone else would have. And maybe those people wouldn't have had the ability to figure out what was going on, or resources to defeat it. More people could have died. So as sorry as I am that you have to deal with this, Ami, I truly believe that Patty, that we, can defeat this curse."

"And if we can't, we'll just have to have the house condemned," Bobbi said. She grinned at Ami to let her know she was kidding.

The friends all laughed, but there was a tinge of nervousness to their laughter.

Bobbi looked at Patty, "Should we ask your teacher, Ann, for help?"

Patty frowned. "No. I don't think we should involve her, but don't ask me why. I just got a strange feeling when I considered it earlier. And I don't think we should have anyone there that we're even slightly uncertain about being able to handle what we will have to do."

Jennie nodded and grabbed the books. "I'll get these and when we have everything, we can just tally it up. Everyone pay what you can towards this. Okay?"

"Sounds good to me," Lyn said.

Jennie stood in line. When she got up to the clerk, he raised an eyebrow and looked at her. "Conducting some sort of occult rite, are you?" He had a really sarcastic tone.

Jennie gave him a look that would freeze fire. "Why do you ask?"

He stepped back. "You're buying three books. Seems a reasonable question."

Perhaps if the clerk had sounded like he believed or had information, Jennie would have responded differently to him; however, he had acted like she was nothing more than a silly school girl. "You might want to mind your own business," Jennie said. He rang up their order and handed her the bag without any further conversation. Jennie was still bristling at him when she got back to the rest.

"He was making fun of us," Jennie said.

Patty shrugged. "You get rather used to it. People either believe or they don't. And there isn't much you can do for those who don't believe."

Ami looked at her. "If I didn't believe in the psychic stuff, would this curse go away?"

"No. It's real," Patty said. "Your mind would just spend a lot of time looking for the so-called rational explanations, and meanwhile, these things would still be happening to you and your family. But because your mind is closed to the possibility of the supernatural, you would be refusing to look for other explanations. The bottom line is this: you'd die because sooner or later, something would happen and you'd say or think something that would get you killed."

"Oh," Ami said.

"I know. You were going to do your best to stop believing, weren't you?" Patty said.

"If it would end that curse, yes. I would be willing to give up that belief."

Patty grinned. "So would I. But I'm glad you're open-minded enough to take me at face value. All of you are," Patty smiled at her friends. "Your friendship means so much to me. I love the fact that you don't judge me, that you believe me when I say strange things. That you never question me or tell me I'm crazy...well, unless you'd tell someone else the exact same thing. It's very important to me."

Ami smiled. Jennie reached over and hugged Patty. Bobbi, Lyn and Ami joined her.

After their group hug, Ami looked at Patty. "What's next?"

Patty looked at her. "We go to a shop that specializes in herbs.   There are a few that we need. Some will help us to protect the house after the curse is lifted. Some will help us to send the curse back to the caster--and with any luck we won't have to deal with her."

"You're really afraid of that, aren't you?" Ami asked.

"Yes, I am." Patty looked hard at Ami. "And you should be, too. Think about the power it took to cast that curse. Think about the evil it took to come up with such a curse. And to cast it not just on whoever her initial victim was, but to leave it in place so that people who she never met, who never wronged her personally, would still be directly hurt by it, that shows a strong personality--and not one I particularly want to meet. I don't know what kind of person would do that. Do you?"

Ami shook her head. The others were watching Patty, clearly getting nervous.

"Patty?" Bobbi said.

"Yes?"

"How dangerous could this get?"

Patty took a deep breath, then looked Bobbi square in the eye. "Very. And to give you an idea of the gravity of this, yes, one of more of us could die from it."

"No!" Ami cried. "I can't let you go through this!"

Patty shook her head. "I can't not do this. Not now. Don't you see? I have to do this. I have to break this curse so no one else is ever harmed from it. It's that important."

"And we will have to give you all the support we can," Jennie said. "All that we can so that it does not come to you or anyone else dying." She added firmly. "None of us will die. Patty is strong enough, and good enough, that she will defeat this curse."

"See?" Patty said. "Jennie's made her mind up, and you guys know what happens when she's decided something."

Bobbi and Lyn said together. "It's done."

Ami laughed. "Okay. Okay. I trust you."

The group drove to a store which sold herbs and other natural remedies. Patty consulted the books while Jennie drove. By the time they found the store, Patty had a list of six herbs that she felt they should get--some were for burning to make an incense to purify the house and others were to use to cleanse, some were for protection for them and some for the house itself.

As they left the herbalist, Patty said, "Okay. One more stop, well, it might be two. Depends on what the grocery store has."

"Grocery store?" Lyn said

"Yes. We need...let me see, right. Eggs, skewers, and candles."

Ami raised an eye brow.

"We're going to make a protective charm," Patty explained.

"Okay."

"And Ami, your dad will have to be brought in. I'm sorry," Patty said.

"Why?" Jennie said.

Patty shrugged. "He's a part of the house, so he is a part of the curse now. If we are to end the curse, we need all of the players involved in it. We're all involved--because of the stories. But your dad brought Sofia into being, so he's a part of this."

"Fine, but he's not going to like it," Ami said.

Lyn snorted. "Um, sorry. It was funny," she said, self-consciously.

Bobbi snickered. "It kinda sorta was, really."

Jennie nodded, "Yeah, because we are all so excited."

Ami finally laughed. "True. I mean...it's just a typical Sunday in Tyler's Falls."

Patty grinned. "So true. Typical Sunday indeed."

The girls went to the grocery store and picked out the items on the list. Lyn threw a bag of Chips Ahoy cookies in the cart. "What? Chocolate is a really strong curative. It enhances positive thinking.

Chocolate chip cookies do it best, in my humble opinion."

Ami agreed, whole heartedly. "Very true." She smiled wryly. "And if I'm going to die, then I think chocolate chip cookies are a good thing to have."

They checked out and got in the car and headed back to Tyler's Falls. They went straight to Ami's tree house to plan.

Patty pulled the books out of the bag. She put them in the middle and took one out. "Feel free to look through these. Maybe one of you will find something I would overlook. Ami, when will your dad be home?"

"Tuesday."

"Great," Patty said. "That's two more days before you can go home. But it's also two days for us to figure out what we should do. How we should tackle it."

Ami nodded. "So we can talk it over for two days, and bring mom in on it. Then Tuesday, we figure out how to tell my dad--and get him to help."

"How is he going to take it, do you think?" Jennie asked.

"Not completely sure," Ami said. "But I'm pretty sure that if he sees Mom, it will help a great deal."

Sofia chose to appear then. "I don't know if it's the best idea to let him see me, dear. He's pretty fragile." She sat down next to Ami. "He has not really gotten over my death, sweetie. I don't know how he will respond to seeing me. I don't know if he would be able to help us if he knew about me."

Ami nodded. "If he thought that breaking the curse would make you go away, he'd have a hard time letting you go, right? Oh, Mom, I miss you, too."

"I know. And I know that it will be hard for you for the same reason, but you must."

Ami nodded. "I know."

"Good girl."

Jennie looked up. "This book says that a curse on an object must have some tie to the caster. Like a drop of blood or a tear or something like that."

"So we have to find that," Patty said. "There's no use doing anything to the house unless we find that." She looked at Sofia. "Can you find the source? We can't go into the house to even look for it."

"I will look. Understand, this curse is old. It might take a while," Sofia said.

Patty looked at her. "You have two days."

"I'll do my best," Sofia looked at her. "I'll be back when I have found them. I don't want to know any more of the plan."

Patty nodded. "Good idea."

Sofia disappeared.

"Okay, good," Patty said. "Now we know we have something of hers to remove. The question is, how do we remove it. If it's a tear drop or a drop of blood, how are we going to get rid of it?"

Jennie shrugged. "What about a wood carving tool? We can carve whatever it is out of the floor, if necessary. Ami?"

"Yeah, right. We're going to do what it takes." Ami said, "And if that's carving a few holes in the floorboards, that's what we do."

"Good."

"Now, Lyn, you're the most artistic of us. I need you to take that dozen eggs, and the skewers. Remove the insides, but don't crack them."

"How am I supposed to do that?"

"I don't know. But figure it out, okay?" Patty said.

Lyn shrugged. "How many do you want?"

"As many as you can make."

"I'm on it," Lyn said. She took the eggs and started to analyze them to see how she could remove the inside without breaking the shell.

"Bobbi, can you go to the hardware store? Please get us the carvers and something to clean the area. It needs to be scrubbed."

Bobbi nodded. "Will do."

"What about us?" Jennie asked.

"We are going to read," Patty said.

"All right," Ami said. They each grabbed a book.

"If it seems relevant, write it down. If it bores you, move on. We're going only on instinct here. Trust it. You will know if it's important or not," Patty said. "When you're done, put it down. Pick up another. We're all going to read them all, because if we're lucky, we'll find what we need in here."

"Why am I not reading?" Lyn asked.

Patty grinned. "Because you will be the one making our protection. You're on defense. We're offense."

"Fair enough," Lyn said. "You'll explain as we go, right?"

"Absolutely," Patty promised.

Jennie started writing down notes from the book she was in. Ami flipped through hers, there was nothing in there that was calling out to her.

Sofia popped back in. "Every room has something in it. Every single room, except the attic. And I can't see it. I could only feel it, so she had to do something that was clear and not noticeable."

Patty nodded. "Thanks."

The girls spent the rest of Sunday at Ami's tree house, and a good bit of Monday, which was fortunately a school holiday. Jennie had no trouble convincing her parents to let Ami stay with them. Jennie's parents were not overly happy about Ami staying by herself, so they were thrilled to have her staying with them while her father was out of town.

On Tuesday, Ami's father was coming home, and the girls were as ready as they could be. Lyn had figured out the eggs. Bobbi had bought the supplies. Now they just had to talk to him and explain what was going on.

Ami's father was not going to be a very happy man; they all knew it. But they didn't have a choice in telling him about it. None of them were really looking forward to the discussion though.

They just had to wait for him to get home.

Chapter 14

After school, Ami and her friends went to the tree house to wait for Ami's dad to come home. Ami didn't want him to go into the house until they had spoken to him.

Finally, after what seemed like forever, Jan pulled up to the house. Ami climbed down and walked over to the car to meet him as he was pulling his travel case out of the trunk of the car.

"Hi Dad," Ami said.

"Hey kid. You miss me?" Jan asked.

"Sure did." Ami looked at him. "I know you just got home, and you want nothing more than to go inside and relax. But, I need you to do something else first. It's important, Dad, or I wouldn't ask."

He set his suit case back down. "You need me right now."

Ami nodded. "Before you go in the house."

"Oh...okay," Jan said, confusion tinting his voice.

He locked the car and followed Ami. She led him to the tree house, and climbed up. Jan followed.

Ami invited him in.

"Hi Mr. Polowski," said Patty and Bobbi.

Lyn and Jennie waved at Jan.

"What's going on?" Jan asked.

"Sit down, Dad. This is going to sound weird," Ami directed. "Where should we start?" she asked Patty.

"At the beginning," Patty said confidently.

"Mr. Polowski, we are going to tell you something. Before we start, I want to say two things. First, everything we are about to tell you is true. Second, we know it sounds insane," Patty said.

"Girls, are you sure we can't wait until after I've had a chance to rest before we do some sort of crazy teenage thing?"

"Dad, this is not a 'crazy teenage thing'! And there is a reason we are insisting on doing this before you set foot in that house!" Ami shouted, taking Jan quite aback.

Jennie looked at him. "Ami hasn't been inside your home since early Sunday mornings. None of us have."

"What happened?" Jan said, fearing there was something terrible in the house.

"That's what we are about to tell you," Lyn said.

Patty started. "You know the local superstition about your house being cursed?"

Jan nodded.

"It is. And this weekend, we found out what the curse was and how it works. We want to break the curse, but you have to be a part of that removal, because you live there," Patty said.

"Girls, this is nonsense."

Patty looked at him. "I did tell you that we knew it sounded nuts, right? Remember that? It's not crazy. We'll tell you all about it, and if we have to, we can bring out something to prove what we've said. We don't want to bring that out unless absolutely necessary though."

"Okay. Go on." Jan yawned. "Tell your story."

"Anything that is said, or thought, or dreamed in that house becomes real. We found this out this weekend when we told scary stories," Patty said.

They all nodded.

"What happened?"

"Fortunately, we...found a way to reverse what happened. But Lyn died. Bobbi was horribly disfigured. It was quite terrifying," Patty said.

"You both seem to have gotten better," Jan said wryly.

"That's because we found out how we could reverse it, Dad, but we need to break that curse," Ami said.

"It's silly, sweetheart. You know that," he said.

"Yeah? It is. But the thing is, when we were fixing the house up, I remember saying 'oh this wall paper comes off really easily.'   And if you recall, I had it all off in one day, right? You didn't think I'd finish that so quickly."

"That sounds like a good thing, though," Jan said.

"It can be," Patty said. "But while you can watch what you say, you can't always watch what you think...or dream."

Ami looked at him. "I don't remember decorating my room. But, I remember a dream where I did it. And when I woke up, it was done. I thought I must have done it in my sleep--but there was one aspect of my room that has bothered me since. All my clothes match my room perfectly. All of them. And they didn't before. That was a part of my dream, Dad. I dreamed that the room was done and it was."

Patty looked at him. "But what if she dreamed she failed a class, or that you died. What if you had a nightmare about someone you know dying or being gravely hurt. That would come true, too.   You can watch what you say--but not what you dream."

Jan looked thoughtful. "Okay. I will accept you believe it. So what are you girls planning?"

"Tonight is a full moon," said Patty. "And that is a good night for casting. Tonight, we are going to go in, remove the physical traces of the curse, perform a purification rite, and place protection charms throughout the house."

"Physical traces?" Jan asked.

"Yes, for the curse to work, the caster had to have a physical link. There are traces in every room of the house, except the attic. Based on where they are, it was like the caster was being given a tour of the house by someone who trusted her." Patty said.

Jan looked at Patty. "You seem to know a lot about this kind of thing." His tone suggested he was accusing her of putting notions into the heads of the other girls.

"I have the Sight. And I've been learning how to use it for six years.   So yes, I do know a lot about this kind of thing," Patty stared him down. "No, I didn't put this idea into the others' heads. This happened. We all saw it. We don't need you to help us find the traces. We do need you to be involved in the purification rite, and the protection rite. And I need you to get rid of those doubts."

Jan looked doubtful.

"Or would you like for us to show you what you have been dreaming of?" Patty asked, quite cruelly. She needed him and they didn't have a lot of time to waste. The moon would be rising soon and the purification rite had to be performed at dawn.

Jan was shocked.

"Sofia, I know you didn't want to see him. But we need you," Patty called out.

Sofia appeared, standing next to Ami. Jan's eyes widened in shock. "Hello, my love."

"How...?" Jan stammered.

"Because you believed you felt my presence in your home. You believed it, so it was true. And here I am. I am part of the reason why these girls survived and were able to reverse the damage of telling their stories. You must believe them. What they are saying is true," Sofia tried to explain it to him kindly.

Jan nodded, tears coming to his eyes. "You're here."

She shrugged. "I'm that part of you. Sofia is gone. I'm your memory of her. Please Jan, you must help the girls with this and there is little time."

He nodded. "All right. What do I have to do?"

Chapter 15

Patty passed around carving tools. "Sofia and I are going to go through the house. She is going to show me where all of the traces are. I will mark them and then we will come back. We'll all go in together and remove these as quickly as possible. I will circle the entire portion that must come out. You will need to carve all the way through the board. It has had years to soak through. You must bring back all parts that you carve out. Everything must come out."

Jan was looking at her.

Patty smiled. "Yes, Mr. P., we're going to tear up your floorboards. Sorry. No matter what, you must bring the wood out."

She handed them gloves. "I don't want anyone getting cursed splinters in their hands."

She stood up and got a bag. She pulled five bowls out of the bag and a jar of salt. Into each bowl, prepared for the girls, she placed a pinch of salt and said, "Protect and purify she who uses you to cleanse her spirit," as she placed the pinch of salt in it. When she blessed Jan's, she said "Protect and arm he who uses you to cleanse his spirit."

She passed the bowls out.

"I'm asking you to perform a protection ritual while I'm gone. This should help keep you safe while you work. Once this curse recognizes what we are doing, it will start to fight back. Prepare for that." Patty explained.

They all nodded. Patty handed out a sheet of paper to each of them. "I've written a protection charm for each of you. They are different. There are instructions on what you need to do to cast this."

"Wait, we're casting spells?" Lyn said.

"Yes. You are."

"But we're not witches or anything," Jennie said.

Patty counted to three in her head. "No. The point of this spell is to place your mind in the right state. Think of it as a form of hypnosis, if that will help."

They nodded and started reading their instructions. Patty climbed out of the tree house and walked to the house. "Sorry about that Sofia, I know you didn't want to see him."

Sofia shrugged. "It was necessary."

They walked into the house. Patty tried not to let her imagination run wild with her, but she did feel like the house was colder than normal. She forced herself to think the temperature was comfortable and normal. Anything she could do to keep the house from using her fear against her, she would do.

Sofia took her to the upstairs first. With a red marker Patty drew circles around every area that Sofia showed her. She could see the stain as she looked at it, now that she knew what she was looking for. In some rooms there were two spots. In the master bedroom there were three. This was not expected; however, it made sense. It just meant that this would take a little longer. By the time they were finished, they had located nine places which needed to be removed.

Patty went to the tree house to get the bag of supplies. Sofia waited in the house. Soon, Patty was leading Ami, Jan, Jennie, Bobbi and Lyn across the lawn towards the house.

Patty stopped about fifteen feet from the steps to the porch. "We're going to cast a protective circle out here," Patty said.

"A what?" Jan asked.

"A protective circle. We're going to be casting some powerful magic, and we need to make sure that nothing comes in to interfere, and that nothing leaks out."

"How do we do that?" Ami asked.

Patty smiled. "Follow me. Ami, you, Jennie, Bobbi and Lyn are going to do the casting. Just follow my directions." She led them to the east side of the house and reached into her bag, pulling out an athame and a book of poetry. These she handed to Bobbi. "The East is the element of Air. It is the sharpness of mind and the inspiration of creativity. I want you to set these items down and read this paper."

Bobbi looked at her uncertainly for a moment. Then she took the paper from Patty. She set down the book and laid the athame on top of it. "I call on the Guardian of the East. I ask you to come to watch over us as we purify this home. I ask your guidance and protection. Let all who enter this circle with intent of peace feel your protection and be blessed by your wisdom."

Patti nodded and led them to the South side. She reached into the bag and pulled out a wand and a piece of coal. She handed these, along with a piece of paper to Lyn. "The South is the element of Fire. It is also passion, love and transformation." The girls all smiled. Lyn was the perfect one to seek the blessing of the South.

Lyn nodded and set the wand and piece of coal down. She read: "I call upon the Guardian of the South. I ask you to come and watch over us as we purify this home. I ask your guidance and protection.

Let all who enter this circle with intent of peace feel your protection and be blessed by your love."

Next they walked to the West. Patti pulled a cup out of her bag and a bottle of water. She handed them to Ami. "The West is the element of Water. It also represents emotion, introspection and dreams." Ami took the piece of paper, the cup and the bottle. She set the cup down and took the cap off the bottle, and filled the cup to the brim. She poured the rest of the water on the earth. Then she read: "I call upon the Guardian of the West. I ask you to come and watch over us as we purify this home. I ask your guidance and protection. Let all who enter this circle with the intent of peace feel your protection and be blessed by the strength of your spirit."

Patty smiled. "You're up next, Jennie."

"I figured as much," she said as they walked to the North portion of their circle."

Patty took out a coin and a stone. She handed them to Jennie. "The North represents the Earth. It is physical surroundings and grounding. This is the foundation of our circle and why it is the last one to be placed."

Jennie nodded. She took the coin and stone and set them down. She read her paper. "I call upon the Guardian of the North. I ask you to come and watch over us as we purify this home. I ask your guidance and protection. Let all who enter this circle with the intent of peace feel your protection and be blessed by your support."

Almost as soon as she finished her statement a feeling of peace and strength surrounded them. Looking up, Ami would almost swear there was a shimmer surrounding the house. She looked at Patty.

"Feel it?"

Ami nodded. No one else did.

"All right. Let's get to this," Patty said. "We have a lot to do tonight."

As they stepped on the porch, Patty uttered a blessing.

"Okay, now, before we go inside, I think we should stick together," Patty said. "And Sofia thinks that we should hum or whistle a specific tune."

"I hope I know it, Patty. Because I'm afraid that Ami and I don't have the same taste in music," Jan said.

"Oh. Something basic. Something we all know. Something that doesn't have any words," Patty said enigmatically.

Ami and Lyn looked at her. Jennie shrugged. Jan frowned.

Finally, Bobbi said, "Well ...?"

"The theme from Jeopardy."

They all looked at her. "You realize we'll hate that song by the time we're done," Jennie said.

"Yes. But there are no words for you to accidentally sing in your head. You'll be thinking about the notes of that song, and thus keeping anything else out."

"Good thinking, Patty," Jan said. "Shall we get on with this?"

"Just one final check. Every one of you did finish the ritual I set out for you, right?"

They all nodded. "Some of it felt silly," Ami admitted.

"I don't doubt that. But it was to create a field of positive energy around you. I just gave you all a spiritual blessing for an additional layer of protection."

Jan stepped off the porch. "Okay, before we go in, I do have one question."

They all gathered around Jan.

"Patty, why do we need all of these blessings and protective rituals now? I have gone in and out of that house, I don't know how many times, since we bought it. We've never needed the protection before."

Patty looked at him and nodded. "Because before you were not going in there with the purpose of removing the curse. The curse was working on you as it wanted to. Now, you're taking an active role in removing it."

"You talk almost as if the curse is a living thing," Jan said.

She shrugged and bit her lip, thinking. "Mr. Polowski, in a way, it is just that. When someone casts a curse on an object, they leave a part of themselves with it. They must, or the curse wouldn't last. That's what we are removing--the part of the caster that she left here. And as we take more and more out, they will become stronger." She frowned. "I wouldn't be surprised at all to see a manifestation before we destroy these pieces. That's why I had you bring those bowls with you--the ones you used for your purification and protection ritual. That's where you will put the pieces of wood that you take out. It will, hopefully, reduce some of the power while we gather them. That's why you are wearing gloves. I don't want you getting any part of her in you."

"You really think we'll see a manifestation?" Ami asked, her voice shaking.

"I don't know. It wouldn't surprise me, but I'm hoping we won't. Because once we gather all of the pieces, we must combine them while we burn them." Patty looked intently at Ami. "But that is part of why you did those protection rituals. To protect you from what might come."

They were all looking rather nervous now. All of the girls knew they needed to be there--they had all been impacted by the curse, and therefore, they needed to be a part of its removal. Jan was uncertain.

"Come on. We must finish removing the physical link before midnight. That's when we must start the next phase," Patty said.

The group entered the house and followed Patty to the top floor - master bedroom. This was the room with the most evidence of the caster. Patty started to hum the theme from 'Jeopardy,' and soon all of them were humming. They all sat down next to one of the marked circles on the floor and took out the tool. Then they started to systematically work to remove sections of the floor.

The first room did take longer, as they each had to learn how to work the tool, get assistance from others, and figure out how much pressure to put on the floor.

Ami had an incident where her piece shattered, and she had to spend several minutes picking up and seeking the small shards. She had finally gone into her room, accompanied by Bobbi, and gotten some masking tape. She had used that to clean the entire area surrounding her segment. She also looked around to make sure that nothing remained.

Patty nodded at her and smiled when she saw the masking tape.

As everyone finished her or his section, Patty checked it, as did Sofia. When they were both comfortable that the section was clear, Patty took out a flask and poured some liquid on a sponge, which she pressed against the wood. She had prepared the mixture earlier. It was oil steeped with sage and rosemary, and she had prepared it while chanting protection and blessings. As she applied the oil, she whispered:

Blessings be upon this floor.
Sturdy, strong, loving support.
No harm allow to pass over you.

The blessing was specifically directed to give the remaining portions of the floor the energy to conduct safe and healthy passages through the house, and banish any of the curse from it.

Finally, Sofia declared the master bedroom safe. They moved to Ami's room, which only had two places. Jan, Ami and Patty worked on the traces in Ami's room while Jennie, Lyn, and Bobbi started with the traces that were in the hallway.

The ceramic surface of their bowls was beginning to change color as more and more wood was placed in the bowl.

"Are we going to finish on time?" Ami asked, breaking the silence.

Patty smiled at her. "Yes, we are. And we're not going to miss any traces of this curse."

Ami and Jan grinned. Patty had apparently decided that if she had to answer a question, she was going to use the house's natural inclination to force statements to come true in their favor.

Patty looked at her watch. They had taken an hour to do the upstairs, but it was completely cleared. They had one trace on the stairs to remove, and a few in the downstairs hallway. And they had a few in the remaining rooms downstairs. They had time. It was still an hour and a half before the time for the next ritual.

The progress seemed to go very slowly, but it was important that everything be removed. Nothing could remain. The curse had permeated the entire house, as it had stewed over the years. All of the surfaces were infected. And this first step was only removing the tumors--the trace elements that secured the curse.

Patty watched as Jan worked on the last of the traces. She had already tested all of the others, as had Sofia, and offered her blessing. This was the last one. He was going slowly and carefully. This was one of the bigger traces. They all were watching intently. Finally, he put the last chip in his bowl and looked at Patty. She closed her eyes to see the aura of the floor. It felt clean to her. Sofia nodded.

As she poured more from her flask onto the sponge, she started to smell an odd smell. She looked around. The wood chips in the bowls were starting to emit something that looked like smoke. Patty shook her head at the others. They had to go out together.

Patty quickly pressed the sponge against the wood. She tried her best not to rush this one or do it partially. This one had to be given the same treatment as the others. However, she could feel a manifestation trying to form around them. She went on with saturating the wood, as she had done on each of the other areas.

Ami gasped. Jennie squeaked, almost as if she were trying to suppress a scream.

Patty looked over her shoulder. There was a cloud of greenish gray forming. It felt very malevolent. The cloud floated through the room to one of the holes, and tried to press its way in. An inaudible shriek filled the room as it met a barrier.

Patty knew she had only a little time left before it recognized that the spot she was working on was the only one that had not been completely protected. She finished sealing it with the oil that she had prepared earlier. She said the blessing one last time. Then she stood up and said, "Gather your bowls. It's time we leave the house."

They each picked up their bowls and headed towards the door. It seemed as if the air had grown thicker, and they felt almost as if it were trying to prevent them from leaving.

Patty took out another bottle of oil, this one prepared the same way but in a spraying container. As they tried to pass, they found it harder and harder to move. The cloud was trying to restrict and suffocate them, as it couldn't penetrate the floor. "Hold tight to your bowls. Do not drop them!" Patty shouted. The spray hit the cloud and sizzled. It backed off. Patty sprayed the floor and walls. "Blessings be upon your surface. Sturdy and Strong, with loving support. No harm allow to pass over you."

The cloud shrieked again. It rang in their minds, causing them to scream.

"Run," shouted Patty.

They all took off running towards the front door and finally got outside. The cloud, however, couldn't pursue. It was fully contained within the house. As they watched, they could see the cloud billowing and filling up the house, its greenish gray mass pressing up against the windows.

Jan looked at the bowl he carried. It had been white when he entered the house, but now it was completely black.

"Patty, why have these changed colors?" he asked.

Patty took a deep breath. "They changed because of the energies we're dealing with. That was why I put such heavy protection on you before we went in. Imagine the psychic residue that it took to change the bowl going into you instead."

They all shuddered.

Patty looked at her watch. "We have just under five minutes to prepare for the next phase. Mr. Polowski, could you and Ami build a fire?"

"I'm already exhausted," said Bobbi.

"Me too," agreed Patty. "But we are nowhere near done. Make no mistake, tonight is a battle."

Jan nodded. He was finally beginning to truly believe. "And we are going to win it." He immediately grabbed some wood and started working on the fire...

Patty smiled grimly. "Yes, we are, sir. Yes, we are."

"So, what do we do now?" Jennie asked.

Patty went over to the tree and grabbed the bag she had set there much earlier. She dug into it, and pulled out a huge white bowl. Patty poured some oil in it. She mumbled some words over the bowl.

"What are you saying?" Jan asked, as he finished getting the fire going.

Patty looked at him. "It's a set of words to help me get in the right frame of mind. They don't have any other meaning."

He nodded.

Patty rubbed the bowl and mumbled again. Then she reached over and took the bowl from Jan and poured the contents into the white bowl. She took his black bowl and smashed it into the fire. Then she did the same with Ami's bowl, then Jennie's, then Bobbi's, then Lyn's, and finally hers. All of the pieces of wood were in the same bowl and all of the black containers were completely destroyed by the fire.

Patty poured the remainder of the oil on the wood pieces in the bowl. "With this oil, I release your bounds from us. Back to your source, I send your ill will." She then reached into her bag and brought out a cloth. It was white linen. She wrapped the linen around the bowl. She poured the oil out into the fire through the cloth. At midnight, she set the bowl in the flames and everyone backed up. The cloth caught fire quickly, soaked as it was from the oil.

They could hear screaming in the house, and turned to watch. The cloud struggled, but started to fold in upon itself. Bit by bit by bit, it grew smaller and smaller. Finally, as the bowl burst into flames, and the last pieces of wood burned, the cloud fit through the key hole and approached the fire.

Patty stood in front of them with her hand stretched out, stopping it. "Return to your caster, and do no more harm here!" she shouted.

It wavered. But Patty didn't blink. She stood her ground, and the others waited with her, holding their breath. Finally, the cloud turned and blew off into the distance. Patty didn't take her eyes off of it until she could no longer see it.

"Is that it?" Ami whispered.

"One more thing," Patty said.

"What's that?" asked Lyn.

"Now, we purify the house," Patty said. "And that we must do until the sun rises. But don't worry. You can actually rest while we do this. And the curse is lifted. But we need to purify the house of the evil that resided there for so long." She grabbed her bag. "Come on."

Patty strode across the lawn to the house. She opened the door and went into the kitchen.

Ami and Jan walked in. It seemed as if the house felt different. There was a strong odor as well. "What's that smell?" Ami asked.

"Residual energy from the manifestation. It won't hurt you, but it's not pleasant. And that's part of what we're going to do now." Patty set her bag down and pulled out several sticks of incense. She handed them out to each of them. She then lit the incense. "Walk around, where ever you feel like walking. While you walk, please read these words."

Patty handed out pieces of paper to each of them. "This is a blessing on the home. It's not magic, just a feeling of well-wishing. Something positive to override the negative energy that has resided here."

Chapter 16

The cloud travelled. It sought out its source, as it had been commanded. It flew over trees, and through streets. But the cloud didn't have far to go. It stormed into the home and wrapped itself around its maker.

Ruth screamed, not in pain or agony. In anger. Shear hatred and anger. Someone had gone to her house, her curse, and had the audacity to tamper with her workings. What kind of an upstart would do that? How? She had spent years perfecting her curse. It should not have been able to be dismantled--not easily. Certainly not using the curse against itself, as she could feel had been done.

She had felt tremors a few days ago, something pulling at her, striking her back. It had felt almost like, somehow, the curse had killed someone--and someone had changed that. How was that even possible? Ruth didn't know, but she felt it might be time to make a visit back there. To set things straight.

She had not forgotten her anger with Diane or with Kyle. It didn't matter that they were both dead. Their house still stood--a testimony to their betrayal. Ruth didn't care that they were dead, or that the current owners had never met either Diane or Kyle. That was hardly relevant. They lived in the house--so they had betrayed her.

Ruth grabbed her cloak and satchel. Whoever had cast back the curse had gotten lucky. Very lucky. But let them...no, let her, the caster was definitely female...try to stand face to face with Ruth and she'd start to understand power. Right before Ruth crushed her, the upstart would understand and fear.

Let her cower, let her beg. Ruth would only laugh. And then she would undo whatever amateurish purification and cleansing that she had done. Ruth was not going to be trifled with, or defeated, by an amateur. What else could she be? Ruth had not felt any new power signatures coming into town. And she knew the power signatures of anyone who had any sort of talent in the arts in this area.

She paused. There had been one. No, that was simply not possible. The last time she had seen her, the girl had barely believed or trusted in any of her basic instincts. The ridicule at school had certainly not helped her confidence any. The girl did not have the knowledge to take out her curse.

Ruth frowned. That was something she should have kept a closer eye on. The situation with her peers should have driven her to Ruth, to learn how to retaliate on those who would humiliate her. But what had happened? Why had that not occurred?

She thought. The friends. The ones that didn't laugh at her, that supported her. "Oh, I should have crushed that. I should have told her that they were only wanting to use her and laugh at her behind her back. That they didn't trust her." Of course, now there is no way that the girl would believe her.

"This is not acceptable!" Ruth screamed. The girl was hers. She was hers. Whoever owned the house on the hill was to blame. The girl would never have had the confidence to take on this curse, not if her friends didn't believe in her abilities. But how? She herself had not believed in her abilities when they last spoke.

Unless the girl had deceived her. Her pupil. The girl she had taught so much to had deceived her. No, it was simply not possible. But Ruth was furious at herself for not seeing how the girl was leaning. But why would she have even looked? She had been planning on seeking her out soon, to give her a stronger taste of the power which was her birthright. Instead, her patience had been repaid by betrayal.

Ruth was as certain of it as anything. She had been betrayed by her student. No one else would have been able to luck into the solution. The girl had excellent instincts, as well she should--given who her parents were.

But how could she have been so stupid? Ruth had trusted him to know what the best path to power for their daughter was, and he had been wrong. She had moved to this isolated town, a town full of people who disliked those who were different. She had abandoned her daughter on the steps of a run-down orphanage. She had given the girl everything she would need to step onto the path of power. And when the girl had started to show the signs of her gift, Ruth had stepped in and taught her.

She was not isolated enough!

This was intolerable. She would go to the house on the hill, and she would confront her protégé, her daughter. And after she had dealt with the occupants of the house, she would take the girl with her. With enough work, she could turn her. Then she could train her protégé up with the correct application of her talents. Ruth couldn't believe that a daughter of hers would have the audacity to undo one of her oldest spells.

Of course, the child didn't know who she was working against. Certainly, if she knew, she would never have turned her back on her own mother.

Ami walked upstairs, slowly, waving the incense in front of her. Softly, she chanted the blessing that Patty had given her.

*"Blessings fill each space with love.
Space below and space above.
Protect those who within here dwell.
Keep them safe. Keep them well.
No matter where they may roam.
Once a house, now be a home."*

It was a simple enough blessing, and thus easy to repeat over and over. While they were walking throughout the house, Patty was placing the egg shells that Lyn had prepared. These were simple protection charms to ward evil from entering into the house.

Last week, Ami would have laughed at the notion that this house had been a shelter for evil, but no longer would she think that. She knew that truly they had been very lucky.

Suddenly, she felt a wave of energy coming towards the house. And while she heard it, she immediately recognized it was not a physical sound.

"Continue what you're doing," Patty shouted to them all.

"What's going on?" Jan asked.

"The person who cast that curse is trying to reinstate it. You must continue." Patty sounded out of breath. She looked very scared. "It will be okay. We have time to finish before she gets here. And right now, our blessing will be stronger than her curses."

Ami felt that Patty sounded more confident about that last statement than she looked. However, she trusted Patty to know what she was doing, so she kept up with the blessing. The house was feeling more light and airy, friendlier, since they had started this. And the putrid smell that had lingered before was breaking apart and being replaced by the light scent of the incense. Ami couldn't quite identify it, but she did like the smell.

When her incense had completely burned out, Ami came downstairs. The others were returning to the kitchen at the same time. Patty smiled at them. She nodded. "I can't feel it here anymore."

"Me, too!" said Bobbi. "It really does feel more welcoming."

They all agreed.

But then another energy wave came up. They almost were able to see it come up to the house, and then be repulsed. "Interesting," Patty said.

"What is?"

"It's closer than I expected. I mean, I knew that the caster would know when the curse was broken.

But, I didn't expect her to be so near to us. She had to live in town." Patty ran to the window, her eyes scanning the road and the driveway.

"What?" Ami asked.

"She's here. It's Ann."

"Your teacher!" Jennie said.

Patty just nodded. "I had a bad feeling about her, and when I thought about asking her, I felt something wrong about her. And that's why I didn't use anything she taught me when we did this. But I never would have guessed she was behind this curse."

Ami pulled Patty to her and gave her a hug. "It'll be fine. You broke her curse. Besides, what can she do?"

"Ami, she put the curse on this house. She's rather powerful."

"And you broke that curse. So are you!" Ami insisted. "Don't forget that, or she'll beat you without even having to try."

Jennie said, "Yeah. She's right. You did this."

"And I have made her mad," Patty said.

Jan looked at Patty. "Well, she has made me mad. This curse threatened my family."

Patty looked at them. "She does not come in this house. Don't let her in."

They watched as the woman they knew as Ann got out of her car and strode purposefully towards the house. She stopped about fifteen feet from the door, where the circle had been cast. Patty opened the door and walked out, flanked by the others. "Good morning, Ann. How nice to see you," she said.

"Actually, call me Ruth, if you don't mind. And let's just drop the pretense, shall we? We both know I'm not here for a social visit." Ruth said sarcastically.

"Okay. Ruth. Why are you here?" Patty asked.

"Don't pretend with me, child. You have not the experience. I taught you everything you know," Ruth said.

Patty crossed her arms in front of her chest, "Actually, no you didn't. Otherwise, I don't think you'd have had to come out tonight because I wouldn't have broken your petty little curse."

Ruth hissed. "It's not broken. It will return, I assure you. As soon as you remove your protections, which you will--sooner or later, you will, it will return."

Patty laughed. "I'm not the only one protecting the house. And the strongest protection, I never touched."

Jan asked, "And why would she want to remove that protection, anyway?"

"Because, I'm her mother you idiot. And she is coming with me now."

Patty shook her head. "No, I don't think so."

Ruth just smiled an evil smile. "I didn't say you wanted to. I just said you were coming."

Blood of my blood, I call to you.
Burn, burn, burn.
Pain I give you step by step
Burn, burn, burn.
Come to me or burn.

Patty fell and started to scream. Ruth continued her chant. Ami looked at Jennie. "Get that bottle. The one with the oil. Hurry!"

Jennie ran inside while Ami stared at Ruth. Patty was screaming. Ami knew there had to be something she could do. She turned to Jan. "When Jennie gets back, pour the oil on her, and bless her. Come up with something."

"What are you going to do?" Jan asked.

"I'm going to shut her up." Ami said with a deadly calm in her voice. She didn't know how she was going to silence the witch, but she had to find a way. Patty's life depended on it.

At the same time, Ami didn't want to hurt Ruth. She was, after all, Patty's mother. And Ami had no doubt that Ruth had something vicious planned for

Patty if true harm came to her. Ruth was not paying attention to the rest of them. She didn't view them as a threat.

And, from a magical point of view, they were not. But Ruth also underestimated them. She thought they would be too scared to do anything, except maybe try to help Patty.

Ruth was wrong.

Ami ran straight at Ruth. She had played a couple Powder Puff football games, and knew how to tackle. So she tackled Ruth and pinned her to the ground.

Patty stopped screaming.

"Stupid girl, I will..."

Ami grabbed Ruth from behind in a chokehold. She left her enough air to breathe, but not enough to speak. "You will do nothing. You will leave her alone--you might have given birth to Patty, but you are not her mother. You're a monster who never cared for anyone but yourself. And I curse you. I curse you with silence, unless you can say something kind or harmless.   You will do no more harm to anyone." Ami had cut herself on the fall, and noticed that Ruth had a cut on her face. She ran her hand across her bloodied elbow and slapped it onto Ruth's cut, holding it there. "My blood is in yours.   A part of me is in you, and you will never hurt anyone again. So says the part of me that will stay with you."

She let Ruth go, and waited. This could go either way.

The others on the porch had stared at her in shock. Patty's mouth was partially open as they all waited.

Ruth opened her mouth, but no sound came out. She reached forward to grab Ami, but couldn't.

Ami stepped back, utterly amazed. She backed up all the way to the porch. "I can't believe that worked," Patty whispered.

"Me neither," Ami said.

Ruth stood in the yard, shocked, and filled with impotent rage. She couldn't move, because she was still trying to hurt the others and think of ways to get revenge upon them. And until she stopped that, she would be stuck.

Chapter 17

A voice came from behind them. "It won't last for long, dear, I'm afraid."

"Annabelle Lee? What are you doing here?" Ami asked.

"Chessie insisted that we come." Annabelle Lee bent down and picked up the beautiful calico cat.

"No! There are no other people in this town with any kind of powers. I would have known!" Ruth shouted.

"It's starting to wear off already, my dear. It was well done, but I'm afraid you don't have what it takes to curse someone. It's just not in your heart."

"What do you mean?" Lyn asked.

"Ami's curse was not a true curse. It was not intended to do Ruth harm. Curses can't change who a person is, deep inside," Annabelle Lee explained. "And Ruth, well, she's just not a happy person. Never has been." She looked back to Ruth.

"You can't be a witch," Ruth shouted again.

Annabelle ignored Ruth.

"What's keeping her right now?" Jennie asked. "I mean, if Ami's curse didn't do anything, what's keeping her from hurting Patty."

Annabelle smiled. "Ami's curse shocked her. That's all it did, and for a moment the shock allowed the curse to take hold.   However, it has been held by someone else since then. But it can't be held in place forever." She looked at Patty. "You must be protected from her. That's partly why Chessie insisted we come. Bobbi, will you please bring the basket that's behind the house to me?"

Bobbi nodded and ran to get the basket.

"Jan, the blessing you put on Patty is holding for now, but soon, the blessing will fade and Ruth will be free. So we must act quickly."

Bobbi returned with the basket, and Chessie jumped down from Annabelle's arms. She ran to the basket and pulled out a kitten. It was a beautiful black and white kitten. She carried her over to Patty. Patty bent down and petted the small bundle of fur.

"Chessie has chosen you for this kitten," Annabelle explained. "She is a familiar. And with a familiar, you will be able to resist Ruth's spells. She won't be able to call to your relationship with her again."

Patty nodded. "Thank you, Chessie. I'm honored." She picked up the kitten and cuddled her close. The kitten licked her nose and purred.

Chessie gave a silent meow to Patty. Then Chessie walked back to the basket and stood guard. She looked over to Annabelle Lee, who looked at Ruth.

Suddenly, Ruth was able to move and talk again. "This isn't over."

Annabelle Lee smiled. "It is for tonight. And Ruth?"

"What!" Ruth snarled.

"You're right dear. I'm not a witch," Annabelle said with a smile. "I'm a familiar. And this is the witch." Chessie hissed at Ruth.

"I will be back," Ruth said.

"I'm sure you will be, and probably very soon," Annabelle said calmly, as Ruth stormed off. She got in her car and drove off, kicking a cloud of dust behind her.

Chessie meowed to be put down again. She went back to the basket and picked up another kitten. This one she carried to Ami and set down.

Ami looked at Annabelle. "I'm not a witch." She sat down next to the little calico kitten, who immediately crawled into her lap.

Annabelle grinned. "No. You're a familiar. This little one is a witch. And Chessie wants you to be her protector. That's really what we do."

"I'm honored. Does she have a name?"

Chessie touched her forehead to Ami's. "She will tell you her full name, in time," Ami heard. "In the meantime, she goes by Trina."

"Trina. That's a beautiful name."

Annabelle sat next to Ami, who was cuddling her new kitten. "Chessie came to me when I was your age. You'll find that Trina will age much more slowly. She'll take about three years to mature to the point where she is able to do anything. And she will tell you her name sometime after she comes into her own." Annabelle scratched Trina's head.

The sun rose. They were certain that the curse on the house had been broken. Ruth's attack had been unsuccessful.

Chessie led the way into the house followed by Trina--Ami's kitten, and Flora--Patty's. After the cats entered the home, Annabelle Lee entered. She seemed to be testing what had been done by the six. She and Chessie conferred.

"It's strong," she finally said, coming back out. "You all did exactly what you needed to. None of us can find any weaknesses. However, the cats are putting a little bit of feline magic into your protections." Annabelle Lee grinned. "No human who does not work with cats will ever be able to break those. They work things a little differently."

"Is that why she never identified you as a threat?" Jennie asked.

"That's exactly why. Well, what are you waiting for, let's go inside!" Annabelle said.

Jan immediately followed her. "It feels--it feels like it's missing something," he said.

"Mom?" Ami whispered.

Annabelle reached out and pulled Ami to her side. "She's gone. But you know that was never her, right?"

Ami nodded. "We couldn't have done it without her, though, could we?"

Patty agreed. "No, because we would never have gotten over the first hurdle. The curse produced her, but it couldn't change her nature." She smiled. "She was your mother, and that meant she had to protect you at all costs." She brushed her hand across her eyes. "She was a good mother."

Unspoken were the words 'unlike mine,' but they all felt them. Yesterday, Patty had no family. Today, she had a mother who had abandoned her--intentionally--so she would grow up an outcast and follow her. Patty's mother had not planned on Jennie, Bobbi and Lyn being the kind of people who would accept her and treat her like family...no matter that she was an orphan, no matter that she had these strange and scary gifts. To them, she was Patty. Their friend. And if anyone was going to be a part of their group, they would have to do so without even questioning Patty at all. As Ami had done.

And because Patty had the support, she was not an outcast.

Still, how could a mother wish such emotional desolation on her child?

Patty thought back to her lessons with Ann...with Ruth. Ruth had frequently tried to discourage her friendship with Lyn, Bobbi, and Jennie. And Patty had always resisted. It was that very action that had made her start to be uncomfortable with her teacher, her mother. And that very action that had made her start to examine what she was being taught.

"I'm sorry that Sofia is gone," Jennie whispered.

Jan looked down. "I just got her back, and now she's gone again." There was utter desolation in his voice.

"I'm sorry, Dad."

He nodded. "I just wish I'd gotten more time with her."

"I'll fix everyone some breakfast," Ami said. "We have school today and you have work."

Jan looked at her. "I'll write you an excuse. You don't have to go."

Ami shook her head. "Jennie, Bobbi, Lyn, and Patti have to go today. Their families don't know what happened last night."

"And I don't want my family to know what happened," Jennie said. "I'm really proud of what we did here, but my family wouldn't understand."

Jan nodded. "All right."

Patty looked at them, "Before we do that, we must Release the Circle. "

"I don't understand," said Jennie.

"We called the Guardians and asked for their protection. When they agreed to come, they were bound to this ritual. We must release them and thank them," Patty explained.

All of them, including Annabelle Lee went outside and walked to the East. Patty handed a piece of paper to Bobbi. "Read this, then gather the offerings you left them."

Bobbi nodded. "Guardian of the East, I thank you for your protection and your wisdom. I release you to return from whence you came, harming no one on your way. If we meet again, may it be in friendship. Blessed be." She bent down and picked up the athame and book.

Patty looked at her. "Those are yours to keep. Find a place of honor for them."

Bobbi nodded.

They walked to the South, and Patty handed Lyn a piece of paper.

Lyn read: "Guardian of the South, I thank you for your protection and your love. I release you to return from whence you came, harming no one on your way. If we meet again, may it be in friendship. Blessed be." She picked up the wand and the coal, and held on to them. "I'll find a place for these."

Patty smiled. Then they walked to the West. Ami took her piece of paper as Patty held it out.

Ami read: "Guardian of the West, I thank you for your protection and your strength. I release you to return from whence you came, harming no one on your way. If we meet again, may it be in friendship. Blessed be." She picked up the cup and poured the remaining water out to the earth.

The group turned to the North. Jennie took the paper from Patty.

"Guardian of the North, I thank you for your protection and support. I release you to return from whence you came, harming no one on your way. If we meet again, may it be in friendship. Blessed be." Jennie bent down and picked up the coin and the stone.

As Jennie picked up the coin and the stone, Ami looked to Patty. Again, she felt the difference as the ritual ended while the others did not.

"Now, we are finished," Patty said.

With that, Ami went into the kitchen, as did the other girls, and started to fix them breakfast. They would have to head home to change shortly, and get ready for school.

After a breakfast of eggs, bacon, and waffles, Jennie drove Patty back to the orphanage and headed to her house. Since Bobbi and Lyn lived in the opposite direction, Annabelle Lee took them home. They planned on meeting back at school. It was going to be a very long day. They were all exhausted, and with mostly lecture classes, it was going to be very difficult not to fall asleep in class. Not that it was usually easy, but today would be harder than usual.

Jan dropped Ami off on his way to work. He decided that if the girls could go to school today, then he could go in to work. Ami had a very hard time leaving Trina, who followed her around, and meowed piteously when she had walked out the door. However, witch kitty or not, Trina would have to get used to not going everywhere with Ami.

Chapter 18

Ami walked to the lockers, and immediately spotted Jennie. "Where's Patty?" she asked. She couldn't say why, but she was worried about Patty.

"Patty said she'd ride the bus, like she always does. So, she should be here shortly," Jennie said. "Look, there's the bus now."

Ami watched as Bobbi and Lyn got off the bus and walked towards the lockers. "Where's Patty?" Lyn asked.

"She was going to ride the bus. Wasn't she with you?" Jennie asked.

"No, when she didn't get on, we just figured you'd waited for her and rode in with her this morning," Bobbi said.

"I offered to do that, but she wanted to keep to a normal routine," Jennie said.

Lyn frowned. "Maybe she sat down and fell asleep accidentally. I mean, we did have a rough night, and she, I think, had a rougher one."

Jennie nodded. "Yeah, she did most of the work."

"And then that thing with her mom. She may have been more tired than she realized," Bobbi said.

Still, Ami was worried. "Jennie, can you drive us over there after school today? I want to check on her."

"Me too," Bobbi said. Patty had been very badly hurt, not just physically but also emotionally, the previous evening. Ami was concerned that she might need some help.

"I hate not checking on her now," Ami said.

The others nodded; however, unless they wanted to answer to their parents for skipping school, they could do nothing until after classes were over.

The day seemed to drag on and on. Ami had to suffer through a pop test in Math and History. Jennie had a disastrous turn at cooking in Home Ec, which resulted in a note to her mother. Bobbi fell asleep during English, and earned a detention. Only Lyn managed to escape the day unscathed.

But it was finally over.

Jennie, Ami, Lyn and Bobbi met at their lockers ready to go check on Patti. At least, Jennie, Ami and

Lyn were. "I can't go, guys," Bobbi admitted sheepishly.

"Why?"

"I got a detention," she whispered.

A chorus of "Why?" "How?" and "Who?" arose from the other girls.

"Fell asleep in English. I didn't mean to, but she just kept droning on about literary something or the other." Bobbi spoke very softly.

This was a surprise to all of them, since Bobbi's favorite class was English, and Mrs. Carson was her favorite teacher.

Ami nodded. She could see that Bobbi was upset about not getting to go check on Patty, and about disappointing her favorite teacher.

"I'm sure Patty's fine," Lyn asserted. "Come to the tree house when you get done. Okay?"

"I'll be there in an hour," Bobbi said.

Since the others were fairly worried about Patty, Bobbi had not asked if they could wait for her.

Jennie led the others to her car and they got in. "I almost feel as if I should go get Trina," Ami said.

Jennie looked at her. "If something is wrong with Patty, I don't know if we should involve Trina just yet. But if there is something wrong, we'll go to Chessie and Annabelle Lee."

Ami nodded. "Okay."

Then Jennie pulled out of the parking lot and drove over to the orphanage. The girls walked up the steps, heading towards the building. Ami saw Flora in the bushes. "I hope they didn't give her a hard time about Flora," Ami said as the kitten rushed up to her, obviously distressed.

Ami picked her up and the girls rushed to Patty's room. Patty was not there. It was apparent she had not been there all day either. There was a sign of a struggle, and Patty was missing.

"Ruth!" Lyn exclaimed. "I'm sure of it."

Ami and Jennie nodded.

"I think we should get Chessie and Annabelle. They'll probably have some information. And maybe Flora does too, but I can't understand her. Chessie will, though," Ami said.

"Agreed," Lyn responded. The three girls ran through the halls, bumping into the director.

"Where are you going so fast?" she demanded.

"Patty is missing. She didn't come to school today, and we were worried about her," Lyn said.

"Patty didn't come home last night," the director said. "I thought she was with you girls, so I was not worried."

Ami decided to take a risk. "Mrs. Raymond, she was with us last night, and early this morning. However, Jennie dropped her off here this morning to get ready for school."

Mrs. Raymond nodded.

"She didn't show up," Jennie continued.

"And there are signs in her room that there was a struggle," Lyn added.

Ami looked at Mrs. Raymond. "We met someone last night who claimed to be Patty's mother. But she and Patty didn't get along well at all, and the woman tried to hurt her. So now, I'm afraid this woman has taken Patty."

Mrs. Raymond looked shocked. "I'll call the police."

"We're going to get someone we think can help too," Jennie said.

"Who?"

"Annabelle Lee."

"The woman who runs the book store? How could she help?"

"Mrs. Raymond, I know you've always been fairly skeptical about Patty's insights," Jennie started.

"True, but if this is what that's about, why not bring over Ann, the woman who has been mentoring Patty for a few years?"

Lyn frowned. "That's a good question. I wish we had more time, but the short version is that Ann is Patty's mother."

Mrs. Raymond nodded, obviously angered that a woman would abandon her child but still watch over her secretly from afar. "You go get your friend. I'll call the police. But I do want a full explanation. Later, all right?"

The girls nodded and ran out of the building.

"When we get to the shop, I need to call home and leave a message for my dad on our machine," Ami said.

"Yeah, me too," Jennie said. "I'm probably pretty grounded, but this is worth it."

Ami nodded. "We might have to tell both of your parents the full story after this. I'm sure my dad will help."

"If that's what it takes to see Patty home safely, I'm in," said Lyn.

"Me, too."

Jennie looked at her watch. "Bobbi should be getting out of detention soon. Why don't we get her on the way to the book store?"

"Good plan. She'd be pretty mad if she got left out of this."

"Hey, so would I," said Ami. "I know I've only known you guys for a couple of weeks, but I feel like I've known you longer."

Lyn grinned. "Going through a life-threatening experience will do that to you. But I agree."

They pulled up to the school just as Bobbi was walking down the side walk. "Hop in," Jennie called. Lyn opened the door, and Bobbi got in.

"Where's Patty?"

Ami said. "We think Ruth got her, and we're going to see Annabelle and Chessie to see if they can help us."

"We should have cut school today," Bobbi said. "We'd be closer on her track!"

"Too late for that. Let's focus on now," Ami said. Flora meowed loudly and Ami petted the kitten.

As they pulled up to the book store, Chessie was waiting on the stoop. She looked hard at them and then wandered to the door. Ami opened it for her and they all went in. Annabelle Lee was already grabbing her bag.

"Chessie tells me we have a problem?"

"Yes ma'am," Jennie said. "Patty's missing."

Annabelle picked up Chessie and followed them out. She got in Jennie's car with them, and Jennie drove towards the orphanage. Flora snuggled next to Chessie, and the two seemed to be having a conversation.

"Where is Trina?" Annabelle asked.

"She's at my house," Ami answered. "Do we need her?"

"Chessie would like us to bring her."

"It's on the way, so we'll make a stop," Jennie said.

Patty glared at Ruth. "What do you want?" She was strapped to a pole and couldn't move.

"I want the daughter you were supposed to be. I set you on a path and you will follow that path," Ruth said.

"I won't," Patty declared with false bravado.

Ruth smiled maliciously. "That's what you think."

"Who is he?" Patty asked. She looked at a man who was setting up something. It looked complicated. As she watched, a very unexpected shape began to take form. She was amazed, because this didn't look like something one person should be able assemble alone.

"Oh, him?" Ruth indicated the man. He was old. Older than anyone who Patty had ever met. "He's just your father. More importantly, however, he is the Operator."

"The Operator?"

"Yes. You are going to go on a ride, my dear." Ruth glared at the man. "Would you hurry up!"

He stared back at her, and the anger between them seemed almost palpable. "This takes time to set up."

"A ride? I don't understand."

Ruth laughed. "Of course not. But it will change the course of your life. You could have done this the easy way. Come to me on your own. But now I will have to redirect your path."

"With a ride?" Patty was flabbergasted.

Ruth just smiled. "Just wait." She looked over at Patty. "And after the ride, we'll be through with all this unpleasantness. It's really quite simple. You ride and I will let you go."

Patty was confused. "I ride some ratty old ride and you'll let me go. You kidnapped me to make me ride whatever he is trying to assemble." She nodded. "Oh, I get it. It'll break while I'm on it, killing me.

But you'll be absolved of the psychic stain of my death since it was not done by your hand. It was an accident." She shook her head. "I'm not getting on that thing. If you want me dead, you will have to do it yourself."

Ruth hissed at her. "If I wanted you dead, you interfering pain in the neck, you would be dead. Daughter of mine or not. No, I want my protégé, and you're going to ride that Ferris wheel, willing or not."

Patty just stared at her. She looked back to the wheel that was slowly going up. And as she did, this time, she could see the evil interlaced with the wooden spokes. Riding that might strip her of who she was--unless she was able to fight it. She was not so sure she could. Patty looked at Ruth and wondered. Had she ridden it?

"How old were you?" Patty asked suddenly.

"What?"

"When you gave up your soul. How old were you?"

"I never gave up my soul," Ruth stated.

"Yes. You did. I can see it now. You rode that...that thing, and gained your power. But there was a cost wasn't there.   You gave up your family. You gave up who you were."

"I was always this," Ruth shouted at her. "Always. I was just waiting for it to be awakened."

She stormed close to Patty. "And you are the same. It's as much a part of you as I am."

Patty shook her head. "I rejected that part of me. I want to help people. I always have. We were never the same. You gave birth to me but you are not my mother." Patty's voice shook with fear.

Ruth glared at her and stormed over to the man. Patty watched her. She was afraid that if she got on that thing she would lose herself. She was not sure she was strong enough to resist whatever power it held.

Annabelle Lee sat with Chessie; Ami sat next to her with Flora and Trina in her lap. Annabelle looked at the police officer. "She is near a carnival. I don't know why, but I'm seeing a Ferris wheel nearby. Do we have any notion of where the nearest carnival is?"

"This is ridiculous," the police officer said.

"Sergeant Tindal, I don't dispute this. But have you anything else to go on right now?" Annabelle asked him.

"No."

"Then could you check where there are carnivals, or have recently been carnivals, near here? This is important."

"All right." Sergeant Tindal called Dispatch and asked the office to start looking for nearby carnivals. The dispatcher told him she would check into the records for applications for licenses and get back to him.

Meanwhile, the cats were still conferring. Ami sat rigid as she tried to give Trina anything she could.

"It really can't be that far away. I mean, she's only been gone a few hours," Ami said.

They all started to think. Suddenly Lyn shouted. "I remember, when we were at the mall. I saw a flyer for a carnival. The flyer was over by the Orange Julius."

Sergeant Tindal called Dispatch again. Dispatch got on the phone with the mall, who sent a security officer over to the Orange Julius to look for the flyer. Ten minutes later, she called back with a location.

"There is a carnival this weekend in Cedar Creek, about three hours from here."

"Good job, Lyn!" Ami cried out.

Chessie nodded.

The girls and cats all jumped up and started to head out of the room. "Where are you going?" Sergeant Tindal asked.

"Cedar Creek," Annabelle replied.

"This is a police matter."

Annabelle looked at him. "It's your jurisdiction, yes. But, you are out of your element. Trust me on this."

He glared at her. Chessie growled and suddenly levitated up to the level of the officer. Annabelle smiled at the cat. Then she looked back at Sergeant Tindal. "I respect you don't believe. But the woman we are dealing with is a witch. You will need someone who can deal with her."

"Fine, but stay out of the way."

Annabelle inclined her head as if acknowledging him. Then they ran down to Jennie's car. Jennie started the motor and drove. "This is a really long day!" she said. "Ami, Annabelle, why don't you two take a nap while I drive. Lyn, you'll have to keep me company."

Lyn nodded.

Ami started to protest when Lyn cut her off. "Jennie and I are just along for the ride. But you and Annabelle might have to do something to help Patty. So you need some rest. Okay?"

Ami looked upset, but Annabelle put her hand on her shoulder. "Your friends are right. It will be you and I who will need our energy. And they can rest before we head back home."

"Look, there's a Ferris wheel," Jennie called out a couple of hours later. She turned onto a road to drive to it.

"Well, most of it. Looks like the thing is still being put together," Lyn said. She turned around and woke up Annabelle and Ami. "I think we're almost here. See?"

Annabelle consulted with Chessie, who nodded. "We are." She looked at Ami. "Are you ready?"

"Not really," she said with a grin. "But I'm sure Patty is more than ready for us."

"That's the spirit."

Ami put the two kittens in her bag, and Annabelle Lee held Chessie. Jennie pulled up to the park. The only ride going up was the Ferris wheel which was rather odd. And in front of the Ferris wheel were Ruth and a strange man. Patty was tied to a pole, watching them put it up.

Ami shuddered when she looked at the Ferris wheel. "There's something wrong with that thing," she said to Annabelle.

"Yes, there is," Annabelle said, frowning.

Ruth and the strange man were ignoring Patty. Ruth was yelling at him to hurry up and finish assembling the wheel and he was yelling at her to leave him alone. And that meant they were not paying attention to Patty. Ami eased towards the pole, moving as silently as she could.

Annabelle Lee set Chessie down and the two of them walked towards Ruth and the man. Then they waited for the bickering to stop, neither drawing attention to themselves nor trying to hide.

Patty was startled when someone appeared behind her. "Shh, just me, Ami," Ami whispered. "I'm going to try to get you loose."

Patty nodded and said nothing while Ami worked at the knots. She watched Annabelle and Chessie grounding themselves to the earth, and taking power into themselves. Clearly, they were preparing for battle.

Once Patty was free, Ami handed her her kitten. "Chessie wanted them here. I'm sure she had a reason."

"I was worried about her. Ruth tossed her out the window," Patty said as she hugged her little familiar. "Let's go," she said, walking towards Annabelle and Chessie. Patty stood next to Annabelle, Flora by her side. Ami stood next to Chessie, with Trina by her side.

"Ruth!" Annabelle shouted.

Ruth turned. "You!" She then noticed that Patty was free and standing next to Annabelle. "What are you doing here?"

"Stopping you, Ruth. It's time someone did. This can't continue. Too much harm has come to pass."

"So you, two kids and three cats are going to stop me? Don't make me laugh."

"You were given a chance yesterday, Ruth. Ami gave you a chance to do no more harm. You didn't take it. Now, we must step in," Annabelle stated. Chessie moved and stood in front of her familiar.

"You wouldn't hurt me," Ruth said.

"No, I wouldn't. But I'm just the familiar," Annabelle said ironically. Just then, an electric charge surged forth from between Chessie's paws and moved straight to the control console for the Ferris wheel. Lightning lit up the panels as electricity danced across it. Within moments, a charge jumped from the control console to the wooden structure itself, striking one of the metal pins holding it together and igniting a flame. The old man tried to protect his ride but was struck and held by the lightning. He screamed in agony as electricity coursed through his body. Soon, he was nothing but a pile of dust.

Ruth screamed as the Ferris wheel burned. She seemed to shrink, to diminish. And as a final strike, the Ferris wheel sent a line of fire straight to Ruth, just before it exploded.

Ami and Patty turned to Annabelle and Chessie in utter shock. "What?"

Annabelle sat down. In front of them, small pieces of the Ferris wheel continued to burn. "I think, and this is just what I've gleaned from Chessie, that the Ferris wheel was how she became who she was."

Patty nodded. "I thought it would steal my soul if I rode it."

"Probably. It certainly took hers. And I think the source of its power was the man she was arguing with. His death is what caused the Ferris wheel to start to lose stability, and his death caused the final strike against Ruth. They were tied together."

"I'm sorry, Patty," Ami said.

"For what?"

"Your mother's death."

"She was never my mother," Patty said in a dead tone. "She gave birth to me. But she didn't give me life, or love. She was never my mother."

Epilogue

One Thursday, a couple of weeks after Patty's kidnapping and rescue, Jan Polowski walked up to the door of the children's home and knocked. Mrs. Raymond opened it.

"Thank you for agreeing to meet with me, Mrs. Raymond."

"Certainly. What can I help you with?"

"I want to adopt Patty Smith."

Mrs. Raymond raised an eyebrow. "Have you spoken with her about it?"

"Not yet. I wanted to find out what I needed to do, and get all of the preliminary work done first. If it turns out that it won't be possible, I don't want her to be disappointed."

"Come on in, let's talk a bit."

Mrs. Raymond led Jan to her office and they sat down.

"The most important thing I want to know, before we go any further, is why you want to adopt Patty."

Jan paused. "I think she deserves a family, and I can give her that. She's smart and strong. She's got a lot of compassion. She's brave. Patty and Ami, my daughter, get along like sisters. Ami has always wanted a sister, truth be told."

"What do you know about her?"

Jan smiled. "I know the people of this town think Patty's a bit odd. That's okay. Odd isn't bad. Uniqueness is important. She is who she is and she doesn't hide it to fit in. Her mother abandoned her, and stuck around, as you know. And just tried..." he paused. "Let's just say that I feel that now, especially now, Patty needs and deserves a family who can love her. She's going to want to go to college, and I highly doubt the state can support that. She's getting close to aging out of the children's home. I know most people don't want to adopt kids her age, and that's all the more reason why they deserve it. You have done a wonderful job with her, Mrs. Raymond. Please know that. I think you do a great job here. You take care of and raise these kids, and I've seen the way other children's homes operate. You run this place like it was your home and they were your kids. These kids need that. But, they also need a family."

She nodded. "Thank you. I can see you're really passionate about this. Does Ami know you're here?"

"I haven't told either of them. And trust me, this isn't just going to be my decision. There will be conversations between me and Ami and me and Patty, and Ami and Patty...and of course all of us. We'll make this decision as a family. The hardest part is not going to be what we think of it. It's going to be what the legal system thinks of it."

"That's true. And we can get you signed up to foster while the adoption process is going through. Just so you know, this isn't like adopting a puppy. It takes a while."

"Right. First step is getting approval to foster?"

"Correct. And I should warn you, approval to foster is a lot easier than approval to adopt."

Jan grinned. "Patty is sixteen. Once she's an adult, it's a lot quicker, right?"

"Right. Very few adoptions happen after the age of eighteen, but they do." She frowned. "I do have to warn you, it's possible that it could take that long."

He nodded. "How long would it take to be approved to foster?"

"It's a lot easier. And because your daughter and Patty are friends, I can even approve you immediately for extended home visits while we complete the foster application process."

"That's great. So I could talk to them about this tonight." He paused. "One other thing. You know I'm a widower, right?"

"Yes. And I have to be honest, that is your biggest hurdle. You're a single father, new to town. The state doesn't like to approve adoptions for single parents."

He nodded. "That's why I wanted to talk to you first, Mrs. Raymond. I'm not about to go marry someone just so I can adopt Patty. I'm not, if the truth be told, anywhere near ready for that. I still feel like I just lost my wife. It's been two years, but it feels like yesterday." He didn't mention that he had recently seen his Sofia and now felt her loss almost as keenly as he did after she had first passed.

"Before we do have Patty come over for the extended visit, I do want to talk to both girls. If they don't want this, then I don't want to force it on Patty. She's been through enough. She doesn't need this kind of rejection added to it."

Mrs. Raymond smiled. "Let's start the paperwork for the extended visit and your foster application, that way when they say yes, you can just pick Patty up."

"Sounds great!"

When Ami got home from the Jennison's that night, Jan was waiting. "Hey, Ami. Before you go to bed, I wanted to talk to you."

"Sounds serious, Dad. What's up?"

Jan sat on the couch and indicated Ami should sit too.

"I'm thinking about adopting Patty. What would you think about that?"

"You can do that?" Ami asked, excitedly.

"Maybe. I can start the process. I've already applied to be a foster parent for her. There's no guarantee that I'll pass the check. Single dad and all."

Ami nodded. "I would have thought that, too."

"But, we can have her over for an extended stay while the foster application is being processed. And after I've been approved as a foster, then the adoption application can be started. It's going to take a while." He looked at her. "But before we do any of that, I wanted your opinion. This impacts you a lot, and I know I have a tendency to do things without thinking about how it will affect you."

Ami grinned. This was true. She was here because of that.

"I'd be thrilled to have Patty as my sister. And this place is big enough, she could have her own room, right?"

"Of course. If she says yes, we're going to paint it whatever color she wants, and let her pick out furniture, too. Just like you got to."

Ami smiled. "It wasn't that I didn't want to share a room with her, Dad. It's just that she's used to having her own space and so am I."

"If she's coming, she'll be treated just like you. She will be my daughter, your sister, family."

"When can we ask her?" Ami asked.

Jan looked at his watch. It was 9 o'clock. "Let's check."

He walked over to the phone and dialed Mrs. Raymond's number. He was slightly surprised when she answered.

"Mrs. Raymond?"

"Good evening, Mr. Polowski. How did your conversation with Ami go?"

"Really well. We were wondering if we could come talk to Patty tonight."

"I thought you might. She's in her room. I'll let her know she's about to have some guests. Just so you know, we don't usually allow guests this late."

"We know. But you know Ami is going to want to tell everyone tomorrow at school if Patty accepts. And it would kill her to keep quiet until after I got home from work."

"Dad!" Ami protested in the background. Jan heard Mrs. Raymond try not to laugh.

Jan hung up. "Ami, I'm going to ask Patty. If she says no, and she has every right to, how is this going to impact your friendship?"

Ami thought. She shrugged. "I'll be hurt, but I'll get over it. She's my friend. It's her choice, and if she doesn't want to do this, it's not about me." She frowned. "But I really hope she'll say yes."

"Me, too, sweetheart. Me, too. Do you want to drive?"

"Boy do I ever!"

The two piled in the car and drove over to the children's home. Mrs. Raymond was there to greet them. "I don't want the other children realizing Patty has a guest. She's waiting for you in my office."

Jan nodded. "I'll talk to her first, alone."

Ami smiled. "I'll wait outside."

"Nonsense, dear, you'll wait with me in the kitchen," Mrs. Raymond said.

"Thanks."

While Jan was talking to Patty, Mrs. Raymond wanted to get a feel for Ami, and how she really felt about this. She didn't have to even ask a question. Ami was clearly excited. She couldn't talk about anything but having a real sister, and helping her set up her room, to raising their kittens together. Ami wasn't concerned that Patty would only live there a couple of years. She was talking about long after they moved away from home. As far as Mrs. Raymond could tell, Ami already considered Patty to be a sister of sorts, and this would just seal it.

Patty stood up when Jan walked into the room. "Mr. P. It's nice to see you."

"Hi Patty, have a seat. I wanted to talk to you."

Patty nodded. "Did I do something?" The girl was clearly nervous.

"No. I have."

"I don't understand."

"I applied to be a foster parent. Specifically, your foster parent. I would like to adopt you, if you'd like. I know we only just met. But I think you'd be a wonderful daughter. You deserve a family. Ami and I would like to be that family." He paused. "You have every right to say no. Ami won't hold it against you. I do know she's very excited about this."

Jan paused again. "And you should understand, I may not be approved to foster. I may not be approved to adopt. I'm a single dad. I'm new to the area. They may reject the application entirely."

Patty smiled. "You want to adopt me?"

"Yes. I do. You're a brave and resourceful young lady. You're very responsible. You and Ami are a good match, and I think you'd be great for each other. I think you'd be a great addition to our family, and I hope you'd find that to be the case for you, too.

"I do want you to know what this means. You'd get your own room--which you can decorate however you like, within reason," he added with a Dad-like pause. "If you want to go to college, I'm going to do everything to make that happen."

Patty felt her jaw drop. That was a dream of hers, and it was not going to be easy as an orphan.

"You'd help me with college, even though we just met?"

"Why wouldn't I help my daughter with college?" Jan asked. "If you agree to this, you're agreeing to be my daughter. That means the standard rules and helicopter parenting. I'll embarrass you just as much as Ami. That's all part of the deal," he finished. "What do you say?"

"Where do I sign?" Patty asked as she ran over to him and hugged him. Jan smiled and hugged her back.

He looked at her. "Like I said, I might not be approved. I'm a single dad. That said, if the courts don't approve it before you turn eighteen, then it's your choice and I'll file that paperwork on your birthday if you want. I don't care what the courts say. That's just a piece of paper--an important one that I want you to have--but it isn't what makes us a family. Deal?"

"Deal," Patty said, her eyes glistening with tears.

"Wanna go tell your sister?"

"Can I? "

"She's in the kitchen with Mrs. Raymond," Jan said.

Patty darted out of the office and ran to the kitchen. Ami looked at her with a hopeful smile.

Patty rushed over to her and hugged her. "So we're going to be sisters?"

Ami laughed. "Yay! You said yes. I really wanted you to."

"Your dad is amazing," Patty said.

"Mine? He's yours now too, Patty," Ami said.

"He is, isn't he?" Patty said back as Jan came into the kitchen.

"That I am." He looked at Mrs. Raymond. "Okay, that's a lot of excitement for one night. Should Patty spend the night here or with us? She and Ami can bunk up for a few nights until we get Patty's room ready, if they want. I doubt either of them is going to sleep tonight, anyway."

Both girls giggled.

The next day at school, Jennie was waiting at the bus for Patty when Ami pulled up and parked her car. Patty and Ami both got out and walked up to her. "What are you doing, Jennie?"

Jennie turned. "Waiting for...Patty, why aren't you on the bus?"

"Ami drove me in."

"That's a bit unusual. You live in the opposite direction."

"Not anymore," Ami said.

"Did you move, Ami?"

"No," Patty said. "I did. You want to tell her?"

Ami shook her head. "I think you should."

"Will somebody tell me something?

"Ami's dad wants to adopt me!" Patty almost shouted.

"Our dad," Ami corrected, causing Patty to laugh.

"I'm a little new to having a dad," Patty said.

"I'm a little new to having a sister," Ami answered.

"Are you serious?" Jennie asked, excited for her friends.

"Yeah, he still has to go through all the formal channels, but he said that even if they said no, we'd do it on my eighteenth birthday."

"We're going to Mill's Valley this weekend to shop for furniture, so that Patty can have the room of her dreams!" Ami said.

"'Within reason,'" Patty quoted with a giggle.

"That is just wonderful," Jennie said. "Who else have you told?"

"You're the first. Let's go find Lyn and Bobbi!"

"Right!" Ami said. "Because there's going to be a slumber party at our house this weekend."

"No scary stories!" Jennie said.

"No, this time, we get nothing but happy endings," Patty said.

About the Author

Cat Francis is an Air Force Brat who currently lives in Hoover, Alabama with her husband, John, and five cats – Thames, Logan, Peri, Jazzpurr and Junipurr. This is her first novel.

Cat enjoys reading, board games, and movies. She also reads Tarot.

Made in the USA
Middletown, DE
05 July 2018